# Broken Orchid

## By

## Tom Snow

In memory of the children of the world that have had their childhood's stolen and

have been lost to Human Trafficking

2

## Chapter 1

*A wall of heavy Fog spreads out in front of me. I see bright lights in the fog. I hear Strange sounds and people talking but can't understand them. I try to turn my head and look around but can't move. I try to raise my hand but can't. I try to talk but nothing comes out. It's growing dark, darker and now it's all moving away from me. Darker and now only darkness and silence around me.*

My name is Mei-Lan and I was a baby when Hong Kong was turned over to the Chinese government. I grew up with my Dad, Mom and my brother Bo, who was three years older than me. We lived in the high rise slum areas of Hong Kong. When I was little, Mom was always at home with us and dad worked for a construction company as a general laborer. We didn't have much money but were better than some. We lived in a two room apartment with a small kitchen and our own restroom, which was nice. We didn't have a bath area so we used a public bath.

Dad was hurt in an accident, on the job, when I was five. He was in the hospital for a long time and when they brought him home they carried him up four flights of stairs to our apartment. He couldn't walk and that's when mom had to go to work at a small restaurant washing dishes and cleaning tables. Since dad was unable to work and mom didn't make much we had to move into a smaller one room apartment with no restroom or kitchen. We had to

use a public restroom on a lower floor and had a little two burner stove for cooking. Mom and

dad had a mat on the floor on one side of the room and Bo and I had a mat on the other side of

the room. I went on the streets with Bo at the age of five to beg for money. We didn't make a

lot but I guess every little bit helped. Every night Mom would bring scraps from the restaurant

for us to eat.

As I grew up on the street, I became street smart. I learned how to steal apples, oranges

and other things from street vendors. There was a magazine stand in front of the hotel where

we would sometimes beg and I would steal magazines from there stand. I couldn't read them

but I loved to look at the pretty pictures in them. Some of them were in English and had

pictures of big houses and people dressed in really nice clothes. I used to think how nice it

would be to live in America and have a nice house, nice clothes and not have to beg for money

and food on the street.

Bo and I became very close on the street and he always watched out for me. He wasn't

just my brother but was also my best friend. Sometimes other kids would try to take our

money but Bo would be so brave and stand up to them and fight to keep it. I was always scared

for him but he would always tell me not to be scared because he would always be there to

protect and take care of me. He would say, he was my special protector, just like the great

Bruce Lee.

Every day we would go home and Dad would be on his mat and seemed to grow weaker

each day. He couldn't walk to the bathroom downstairs so he had a small pot next to his mat that he used for a restroom.  Many days we came home and his mat would be wet with urine.  Bo and I would clean him and his mat and try to make him comfortable.  He would always pat Bo on the head and tell him how proud he was of him and how he knew Bo would grow in to a great man.  He would hug me and tell me how much he loved me and how pretty I was just like a beautiful orchid flower.

Mom would always come home after dark with a sack full of scraps from the restaurant and we would sit on the floor next to dads mat and enjoy our food.  She would always get up early, fix food for dad to eat and leave it next to his mat.  I don't remember her ever having a day off.  She worked so hard and was growing old so fast.

*The fog is so thick around me and I can see lights in it.  I can hear talking but don't understand it. I try to move but I can't.  I try to talk but nothing comes out.  It's moving away from me and it is growing dark, dark and darker.  Now it's only darkness and silence around me.*

One day Bo and I walked further into the business district away from the slum area.  There were tall buildings with beautiful gardens around some of them, full of pretty flowers.  Bo said they were banks full of money for rich people.  I saw lots of nice cars and people wearing really nice clothes.  We had been there almost all day and had done great.  Suddenly someone grabbed us, from behind, by our hair.  It was a police officer and he threw Bo on the ground and put his foot on his chest holding him down while holding me by my hair.  He took all of our money and told us to go and if we ever came back to his area he would put us in prison for the rest of our lives.  We took off down the street, when he released us and I don't know what was faster, my heart or my feet.

A few days after that we were begging in another area when some boys came up to us and demanded our money.  Bo got in a fight with one of them while another held me.  Bo didn't have a chance, there were too many of them and they beat him up really bad but I think his pride was hurt the most.  I helped Bo home and he kept telling me how sorry he was he had let me down and lost our money.

I looked at him and said, "Even the great Bruce Lee would have been out numbered." We laughed and cried together all the way home.

One night we came home and was surprised to see Mom sitting in the hall outside our apartment crying.  She hugged us together on the floor and told us Dad had died.  The coroner had already took him away to the morgue.  We sat in the hall together for a long time crying before we went into the apartment.  I remember mom saying everything would be okay and dad was better off because he had gone to a better place.  That night I don't think any of us slept much.

I looked at Bo and said, "Bo, where is the place dad went?"

He looked at me with tears in his eyes and said, "Not sure, but I think you have to die to go there."

We were silent the rest of the night and I lay on my mat thinking about Dad and where a better place might be.  Maybe some place we would have more money, pretty clothes, a big house and lots of pretty flowers around it.  And best of all Bo and I wouldn't have to go on the street and beg for money.

We kept working the streets.  Mom was working longer hours to pay on the loan she

had borrowed to pay for dad's funeral and burial place. Sometimes while working the streets

people would come up to us and start telling us about some guy named Jesus.  They said he had

died and came back from the dead, after dying on a cross, then went into a place called heaven.

They said he died for us.  They said he could make our lives better and was preparing a home

for us in heaven.  I would listen and think that might be good.  Then Bo would pull me away and

tell me not to listen to them because they were crazy and lied to people to get their money.  If

we were walking down a street and they were there we would cross to the other side to avoid

them.  Sometimes I felt like I wanted to hear more about this guy named Jesus and his heavenly

home but Bo would never let me stop and listen.  He would always grab my hand and pull me

away.

On my eleventh birthday I had my first party.  Mom brought home a small white cake

she had brought from the restaurant where she worked and even had a present for me.  Bo

even surprised me with a present wrapped in an old newspaper.  That night we ate the

restaurant scraps and then ate the white cake.  It was great and I was so happy. Mom handed

me her present first and it was so beautiful.  It was a beautiful yellow head scarf and I loved it.  I

was so excited, I laughed and cried with joy.  Mom tied it around my head and hugged me

telling me how much she loved me and I was her beautiful orchid. Bo was so excited for me to

open his present.  As I unwrapped the present my hands were shaking and Bo was laughing. Bo

had found a picture of a beautiful yellow house, with large windows, a beautiful front porch on

it, a white picket fence around the house and flowers everywhere.  He had glued it to a large

piece of white cardboard so it looked like it was framed.  It was the most beautiful picture I had ever seen.  Bo told me that it was the kind of house American people live in and he knew just like Dad had said, I would have a house just like it someday.

From that night on I started day dreaming about going to America and living in that house with my Mom and Bo.  No more begging for money and food.  Just a place we would be better and happy all the time.  I even wondered if that is where you go when you die.  Maybe Dad was there, then I thought I didn't want to die to go there.  I taped the picture on the wall next to my mat and would stare at it every night before falling to sleep and then I would see it in my dreams.

Things went as usual for us.  Mom was working long hours and Bo and I went on the streets every day.  I guess we were happy because we didn't know any better and we had each other.

## Chapter 2

*I hear someone talking to me but don't understand what they are saying. I see an image of a face in front of me but it's not clear, the fog is so heavy. I try to ask where I'm at, but nothing comes out. I try to lift my hand and touch the face, can't move my hand. Now everything is moving away from me and it's getting dark. It gets darker, darker and now only darkness and silence.*

It was a cool day with a light mist in the air when we left home that day. The sky looked like it wanted to bust open and start raining at any minute. I had my yellow scarf tied around my head and felt so pretty. We walked deep into the business district that bordered the slum area, hoping for a good day. I would stop and look at my image in the glass doors as we passed, and yes, I did look good with my long black hair and the yellow scarf tied around my head. As we went around one corner we ran into a group of people on the sidewalk. A white lady was standing on a wooden box talking, I think in English, to a small crowd of people around her. A Chinese lady stood on the street next to her translating what was being said. She was talking about Jesus and how he could save us from the world and he was in heaven preparing a home for us. She said it didn't matter if you were white, black, Chinese or poor because he loved us all and would accept us all into his arms.

Bo kept telling me to come on but I wanted to listen and learn more about this guy and his heavenly home. I stood there and listened while Bo went a ways down the street and started begging. After a little, a police officer came up to the crowd and told them to break up and move along. As they started leaving one Chinese lady grabbed my arm saying, "Child come with us. Jesus loves all the children and we can give you a better home and life."

My heart beat so fast and I started to shake. I pulled away from her and started running down the street. I didn't look back to see if she was following. I just wanted to get away from her. I ran up close to Bo and grabbed his hand then looked back and she wasn't following so I let out a sigh of relief. Bo looked at me with a disgusted look and a frown on his face like he wanted to say, *I told you so. They're crazy.*

We spent the day in that area and it went pretty good. I thought about what the lady had said about Jesus some during the day but eventually put it from my mind concentrating on what we were doing. It was a good day and we did okay. The rain held off with only a light mist, now and then.

We were headed home when the boys approached us. They were all about the same age as Bo, except for one. He seemed much older and bigger than Bo.

There were four of them and they circled around us, with the bigger boy in front of Bo. Bo grabbed my hand and pulled me behind him as the bigger boy got right up in Bo's face.

He grinned and said, "I'll take the money."

Bo threw him a hard stare saying, "No way, we worked for this money."

10

He pointed his finger at Bo, almost touching him, saying, "You're working our area, so it's our money."

Bo squeezed my hand and started to walk around the boy but he hit Bo hard in the stomach knocking him back. Bo dropped my hand and swung at the boy but it was blocked and Bo was struck again. Bo jumped on the boy and they both fell to the street. The boy pushed Bo and pinned him to the street. Bo kept trying to hit him but couldn't move his arms. I tried to jump on the boy but one of the other boys wrapped his arms around me and held me back. Bo was able to break one hand free and slammed it into the boys head. The boy fell to the side but before Bo could stand up he pushed Bo back down and hit him really hard in the chest. I heard Bo gasp and then scream. The boy stood up over Bo looking down at him on the street. Bo said nothing but just stared at the boy. The boy looked around at the other boys then he dropped a knife to the street and started running. The boy holding me released his grip and they all took off.

"Bo, Bo are you okay?" I screamed as I ran to him.

He said nothing but just stared at me, gasping for air. I knelt by him and pulled his head on to my lap. A light rain started coming down and people started to gather around us. Then I saw the blood oozing from his chest so I took off my scarf and pressed it down on the wound, to stop the blood. The rain came heavier and my scarf started to turn black as it soaked up Bo's blood together with the rain. Someone opened an umbrella over us and I heard someone say that help was on the way.

With drops of rain and tears streaming down my cheeks I held Bo close and said, "You'll be okay, you'll be okay. Help is coming. Help is coming and you'll be okay."

He looked up at me with tears in his eyes and with a trembling voice said, "Sorry Mei-Lan. I let you down. I'm so sorry."

I held him tighter as he slowly closed his eyes, he was gone. I pulled his lifeless body as close to me as possible and held him as tight as I could. I covered his face with my chest to keep the rain from hitting him.

As tears and drops of rain rolled down my face I kept crying out softly, "Oh Bo, Oh Bo, no, no, please don't go. Please don't go."

I don't know how long I sat in the rain holding Bo. I don't know when they took him away and I don't know who took me home. I just know I lost Bo, my brother and my best friend, that day on that rain soaked street.

I woke up on my mat in Mom's arms. She was holding me tight and running her fingers through my hair. She was crying and telling me that I was going to be okay and how she loved me so much. I would close my eyes but kept seeing an image of Bo laying on the street in a pool of blood with the rain falling on him. I felt like I had also died on that street and my heart had been cut from my body when I lost Bo.

*The fog around me is so thick and there are bright lights in the fog. Someone is talking to me, I can't understand them. I see an image of a face in the fog. I try to raise my hand and touch the face, my arm won't move. I want to say something, nothing comes out. Where am I and what's going on and who are you? The image starts to move away from me and it grows*

*dark and then darker.  Now it's only darkness and silence.*

Chapter 3

I had turned twelve since the day Bo left me on that street. Mom wouldn't let me work

the streets and I went with her to her job almost every day. She was working even more to pay

on the loan for Dad and Bo's funerals and burial plots. I would help Mom in the kitchen,

washing and cleaning, but they paid us no more, so times had gotten really hard for us. I think

Mom didn't worry about the money but just didn't want me back on the street for fear of what

could happen. I was really worried about Mom. She was aging so fast because I know she was

worried about me and she worked so hard. I missed my Bo so much. Some days I would fake

sickness and Mom would let me stay home with strict instructions about staying in the

apartment. On those days I would sit in our apartment staring at the picture of the yellow

house. My thoughts would go back to the night of the party when Bo gave it to me and I had

been so happy that night. Sometimes I would sneak off to the place where Bo had died. It had

been a year since that day in the rain. There was no shrine or anything there for Bo. As I stood

there looking at that place I could still see an image, in my mind, of Bo laying on that blood

soaked street in the rain. Everything and everyone there continued on just like nothing had

ever happened. But I knew, and would always remember where Bo had left me and a part of

me had also died.

One day as I was helping Mom wash dishes an old Chinese man came into the kitchen and took Mom to the side. As they talked, they kept turning and looking at me. So I knew they were talking about me. As the old man started to leave, Mom bowed to him out of respect. I went to her and asked what was going on. She just said for us to get back to work and she would talk to me when we got home.

When we arrived home that night mom sat me down on my mat. She told me that the old man was Mr. Yun, the owner of the place she had borrowed the money. He was aware of the hardships we had and wanted to help. He worked with some people that placed children in good homes in America. The families in these homes would help the child get an education, learn English and obtain a better life. In return, the child helped around the house by taking care of any smaller children in the home and cleaning the house. Mom said it would be an opportunity for me to go to America, where I would be cared for, get a good education, grow up, find a good job and then she could maybe move to be with me. She said it would be an opportunity for both of us. I had never been to school and I always knew America was a wonderful place because of the pictures I had seen. I told Mom I would miss her so much, so I wasn't sure if I should do it. I told her I was scared to do something like that but she said I would lose that fear once I was there and in a nice home and going to school. We talked about it for a long time and finally agreed it would be the best for me. Mom said she would contact Mr. Yun and let him know, so he could start the process. I had a hard time sleeping that night for thinking about going to America and leaving Mom in Hong Kong. I stared at my picture on the wall and became so excited. Then I would think about Mom and was overcome with sorrow and start to cry. I tried to cry softly because I didn't want to wake her. But I knew it was the best for both of us because she wouldn't have to worry about me so much, even though she probably would anyway. Mr. Yun had also told her that the family would sometimes help pay off the loans that burdened her so much.

The next day Mom notified Mr. Yun that we would do it. Things started moving quickly. We went to his office and he took pictures of me for a passport to send to families in America. He told me I was such a pretty girl that he was sure someone would want to sponsor me. I had been told by many people before that I was very pretty. I didn't think so and thought I was like any other Chinese girl. I had long jet black hair, tall and slender build. I guess I was a little more developed in some areas than the average twelve year old. But I always thought that was maybe something that wrong with me.

About a month passed before we heard from him again. He sent word for us to come to his office. He had lots of legal papers for Mom to sign, giving me permission to leave Hong Kong with someone other than her. He had a passport for me and a letter from a family in America I would be staying with. It was written in English but had been translated to Chinese. Being I couldn't read, he had Mom read the letter to me. It was from a family of four that lived someplace called Oklahoma. The father's name was Ben and the mother was Susan. They had two children, a boy age three and a girl age five. They wrote how they were looking forward to me joining their family. They were excited about helping me go to school and build a new and better life. They said that Ben spoke good Chinese, he had learned while in the army, so he could help me in school. They enclosed a picture of them standing on the front porch of their home. It was so pretty with flowers all around the porch. I was so excited my fear started to fade away.

Mr. Yun took me to a store and bought a small suitcase and a few pretty dresses for my trip. He said it would be about two weeks before I would leave for America. It seemed like everything was moving so fast. When I thought about going to America I was scared and happy at the same time. I only wish Bo could be here to go with me.

About two weeks later, the night before I was to leave, Mom and I laid together on my mat holding each other. Mom cried telling me how much she would miss me but this was the best thing for me. She told me to go to America and work hard, study and make a better life for us. I closed my eyes and before falling to sleep said to myself, *my dream was going to come true.*

The next morning we got up and Mom started helped me get dressed in one of my new dresses and pack my little suitcase. The last thing that went into the suitcase, before I zipped it closed, was my picture from Bo of the yellow house with the flowers all around it. Mom fixed my hair and then surprised me with a new gift. I was crying, tears flowing down my face and my hands were shaking as I opened it. It was a yellow scarf, like the one I left with Bo in the street. Mom hugged me tight and told me how she loved me so much and Bo and Dad would both be so happy for me. We grabbed the suitcase and left for Mr. Yun's office.

We didn't talk much as we walked to Mr. Yun's office at the edge of the slum area. Mom insisted on carrying the suitcase and all I could think about was going to America then I realized I had never been on a plane before and suddenly felt sick at my stomach. I didn't say anything to Mom but just kept walking. I knew I had to be brave because this would give me the chance to make a better life for both of us.

It took about an hour to walk to Mr. Yun's office but it seemed like it went by really fast. We walked into the office and was greeted by Mr. Yun. He turned toward a lady standing by his desk and introduced her to us as Ms. Ming. She was a lady about Mom's age, dressed very nice with perfect hair that was graying slightly on the sides and she wore light makeup. She immediately shook Mom's hand and then hugged me. She was to be my escort to America, along with some other girls also going to different homes in America. She held an envelope with my passport and all the necessary legal papers in it in her hand.

She smiled at me and said, "Are you ready to start your big adventure and path to a new and better life?"

I looked at mom and with a shaky voice said, "Yeah, let's do it."

She gave Mom a hug and told her not to worry because she would take good care of me. She looked at her watch and then looked to the street. A large van pulled up in front of the office and she said it was time to go. I gave Mom a long hug and with tears in my eyes told her I loved her. Mom was crying as I followed Ms. Ming out the door with my suitcase in hand. Mr. Yun stood next to her with his arm around Mom's shoulder, trying to comfort her. The door of the van opened and I climbed in. Four other girls were in the van. They all looked at me and smiled. Ms. Ming climbed into the passenger side of the front and we left.

The next few hours were very hectic and rushed as we arrived at Hong Kong International Airport. Ms. Ming helped us go through security and boarding. She had all our tickets and passports. We all had seats together in the same area on the airplane. None of the girls talked. I think they were scared and in shock just like me and afraid to open their mouths. When we started to taxi and the plane started moving faster down the runway I thought I would throw up.  My pulse was running away and my heart was beating as fast as the plane, as it moved down the runway. I had sweat trickling down my forehead and a death grip on both arms of the seat as the plane started going faster and faster.  I felt a clammy hand grasp mine.

Looking at the girl next to me and with a trembling voice I asked, "You scared?"

She said nothing but closed her eyes gripping my hand tighter as the plane lifted from the ground.  It was a long time before any of us moved or talked.  I think it was a first experience for all of us.  My heart finally started to slow back to normal.  I was very frightened but also very excited.  I closed my eyes and could see Mom, in my mind, standing with Mr. Yun and bidding us goodbye, I already missed her. We had been in the air for a few hours before the girl next to me spoke.

"My name is Su-Lin.  I'm sorry if I squeezed your hand too hard."

I smiled at her and said, "That's okay.  I was scared too. I am Mei-Lan."

I looked around to see Ms. Ming sitting behind us with the other two girls in seats next to her.  The plane was full.  I didn't see an empty seat anywhere.  People were starting to get up and move around talking to each other.  The ladies working on the plane started bringing drinks to people and talking to different people.  I had to go to the restroom so I turned to Ms. Ming and told her.  She motioned for me to come with her but told the other girls to stay in their seats if they didn't need to go.  As it turned out, all of us needed to go, so we paraded behind Ms. Ming to the back of the plane, where the restrooms were located. During the flight Ms. Ming ordered our food and anything else we might need.  At one point Su-Lin and I started

19

talking about our adventure ahead of us. How excited we were. But when we started talking about the families we were going to live with Ms. Ming leaned over the seat and told us that was not allowed. We were not to talk about where we were going or the families we were going to stay with. I thought that was odd but said no more about it.

Su-Lin told me that both her parents had died in an accident so she went to an orphanage for a year before she was adopted by a couple in Hong Kong. Her new parents made arrangements for her to go to America shortly after she moved with them. She said she was very scared but knew Jesus would be with her and protect her.

I questioned her, "You know about Jesus?"

She looked at me with a big smile on her face and said, "Oh yes, my real Mom and Dad were strong Christians and really believed the words of Jesus. I know they are with him now in his heavenly home. I believe in him very much. Don't you?"

I said, "I've heard about him but don't really know him. How do you know he's with you and all that?"

She pulled a small book out of her pocket and handed it to me, "This is my bible and it tells all about Jesus. It talks about his life from when he was born until he died and came back from the grave. Here, you can take it and read it until we arrive in America."

She started to hand it to me but I pushed it away saying, "That's okay, I don't know how to read."

The lights went down low in the plane and Ms. Ming leaned over and told us it was time for us to sleep. I closed my eyes but could not fall asleep for thinking about Mom, America and Jesus.

*The fog is thicker now and glows from the lights in it. I hear strange sounds around me but no one talking. I want to turn my head and look around but can't move. I try to call out to anyone that can hear me but nothing comes out. Now it grows dark again, darker and only darkness and silence around me.*

I'm not sure how long we were on the plane, I think for most of a whole day. After a long time Ms. Ming leaned over the seat, while the airplane lady was talking to everyone, and told us to fasten our seat belts because we would be landing soon. I don't know what scared me more, the takeoff or the landing. I did like the idea that we were going to be back on the ground.

After we landed and came to a stop Ms. Ming gathered us together as we departed from the plane into a big building We were met by a tall man with very black hair and a dark complexion. He wore a uniform with a badge on it so I guess he was a police officer of some sort. Ms. Ming talked to him for a moment and then she handed him the envelopes with our passports and papers. He escorted us to a window where another man looked at our passports and then motioned us to go. They spoke very little, but it didn't sound like English. We followed him out of the building to a waiting truck. He turned and said something to Ms. Ming and then she told us to get in the back of the truck. As I climbed into the truck I thought. *What about my suitcase and my picture from Bo.* Something didn't feel right but I obeyed. In the back of the truck were eight other girls. They were all Asian. The door closed behind us and it became dark. There were no lights in the truck. I couldn't see anything but then I felt a familiar hand grasp my hand and squeeze. Once we started moving we didn't stop for a long time.

The truck finally stopped and the door opened. A different man motioned for us to come. We all piled out of the truck and started following him. It was night and we were on a dock next to very big ship. Another man joined us and started pushing us up a gangplank on to the ship. They were yelling and screaming at us but not in Chinese or English. Not sure what it was. There were containers stacked on the ship and we were pushed towards a large opening on the deck of the ship. They motioned for us to go down a ladder into a large open area inside the ship. Sweat flowed down my face and my back. My heart raced and my lips trembled. I looked at Su-Lin and she had the look of death on her face. At the bottom of the ladder another man with a gun directed us into a large open room on the side. As we entered the dim lit room I could see other girls sitting on the floor. There were maybe thirty more girls in the room. The man motioned for us to sit on the floor with the other girls. Another man came in the door and stood next to the man with the gun. He was Asian and he stood talking to the first man. The first man walked towards us and started talking but I couldn't understand him. Some of the girls, not Asian, started crying and then he turned to look at the Asian man.

The Asian man stepped forward and started talking in Chinese, "We have a long voyage ahead of us. You make no problems and you'll be okay. You can scream, you can cry but no one will help you. You will be fed at different times. If you need to piss or anything find a place in the hole here because you will not be leaving here for about seven days. If you make trouble I will feed you to the sharks."

A man brought in some large boxes and dumped them on the floor.  Bottles of water and an assortment of packaged sandwiches were scattered across the floor.

The Asian man nodded to the other men as they went out the door and then the door closed shut and I could hear them turn the lock on the door.

# Chapter 4

After the door closed I looked around the room at the other girls.  They all were young and the sense of fear and the unknown could be felt in the room.  Some of the girls were grouped together in small groups crying and talking in something other than Chinese.  I looked to Su-Lin sitting on the floor next to me.  She was holding her book about Jesus in her hand, crying, as she prayed to the guy named Jesus.  I pulled my knees into my chest as I sat on the floor and began to shake and cry.

*Fog is heavy and wrapped around me like a great white blanket.  Where am I?  Why can't I move or talk?  What are the lights in the fog?  Who is talking to me?  No, please don't go! Please!  It's getting dark again.  Darker, darker and just silence.*

I had cried myself to sleep.  When I woke my head was laying in Mom's lap.  It had just been a bad dream.  I turned to look up at Mom. But Mom wasn't there, it was Su-Lin.  I sat up looking at her.  Her eyes were red and swollen from crying so much.

My voice trembled as I asked, "What's happened?"

Her voice was shaky, "I don't know, but I think we are in real trouble. I don't think we're going to America and I know something's not right."

I think the ship was moving but not sure. We could feel it at times. The only time we seen the men was when they opened the door to throw food and water in. After what I think was a few days in the heat of the room the smell of urine, sweat and poop was almost unbearable. Some of the girls became sick with a fever but no help came.

One of the girls died from the fever and another banged on the door. Finally the door opened and two men, one with a gun, came into the room. The girl that had banged on the door yelled at them in another language pointing at the body on the floor. The man with the gun looked at her as she was yelling and knocked her to the floor with a swift backhand. The other man looked at the girl, dead on the floor then grabbed her by the hair and dragged her from the room. The man with the gun said something and backed out the door and the door closed behind him.

Su-Lin spent most of her time reading the little book and praying to the guy named Jesus.

One day as I sat next to her, while she was praying I said, "Why doesn't your Jesus help us? Where is he? They say he loves everyone. If he loves us," I paused and cried out, "why doesn't he help us?"

She became so calm and with a smile on her face said, "He already did. He died for us on a cross so we'd have eternal life. I'm very scared but inside I know that my Mom and Dad are in heaven and if I die I'll go to heaven and see them again." Tears rolled down her face as she reached for me and hugged me tight.

As she hugged me I felt a calm come over my body.  I knew in my heart that Su-Lin had something special in her and I was glad at that moment to be with her and I wanted what she had, but was afraid to ask how to get it.

Time went by, I don't how much.  We couldn't tell the difference between night and day.  They kept throwing bottles of water and food into the room.  They never cleaned us or the room so the smell of urine, sweat, trash and other things was horrible.   Sometimes the lights in the room would go out and we would sat and hold each other in the dark.   The other girls, that weren't Chinese stayed together.  The Chinese girls even had their own little groups.  I think we were all between the age of twelve and maybe fifteen.  The smell of fear in the room was stronger than any other smells and I could even feel the fear in the air.

As I laid down next to Su-Lin I placed my hand on her shoulder and asked, "I can see you have this Jesus in your heart and it gives you strength.  How do I get that?  What do I have to do to become a Christian?"

In a very weak voice she said, "All you have to do is just ask and he will come into your heart."

I could see as she closed her eyes she was feeling bad and was very weak.  I thought I would let her sleep and ask her more about it when she woke.  I pulled her over to me and circled my arms around her holding her tight.  I thought about her and Jesus as I fell asleep.

I woke up with my arms still around Su-Lin. She was so hot and was shaking, so I held her tighter.

I asked nervously, "Su-Lin, are you okay?"

She opened her eyes and looked at me. She lifted her hand with the little bible in it and offered it to me.

I smiled and said, "You know I can't read. What do I need it for? Anyway, you may want to read it later."

She smiled and kept pushing the bible at me. I grasped it in my hands and said, "Okay, okay, I'll hold it for you."

She smiled at me with the sweetest smile and closed her eyes. I heard a gasp of air from her mouth and she went limp in my arms.

I pushed her away from me a little and then pulled her back close and hugged her tight saying, "Su-Lin, Su-Lin, wake up, please wake up. Su-Lin, please wake up."

I looked into her face and she looked so peaceful. I knew she had left me, just like Bo, she was gone. As I looked into her face, somehow in my heart, I knew Su-Lin was in a better place. She was with her family and Jesus in heaven. I clutched the little bible tightly in my hand and held it to my heart.

I lay on the floor holding her. One of the other girls banged on the door until the men came in and dragged her lifeless body from my arms and out the door.

I held the little bible next to my heart and prayed the first prayer in my life, "Jesus, I don't really know you but I want to. Su-Lin really loved you and talked about how great you are and your house in heaven. Please take care of her and I want what she had with you."

At that moment I felt as if my fear and a heavy load had been lifted from me. I knew at that moment I had Jesus in my heart and it didn't matter what happened to me because he was with me.

I really missed Su-Lin. I hadn't known her very long but she had become a precious part of my life. I knew she would always be in my heart.

I sat in the room with the other girls. It seemed as if days passed slowly. The only time we seen the men was when they would throw water and food into the room. I just wished so much that I knew how to read, I could pass time by reading the little bible and I had this tremendous desire to learn more about Jesus.

The door opened and the Chinese man came in with the other men. He looked around the room and then smiled and said, "Welcome to America."

He laughed and then told us to follow him out the door and up the ladder. The other men followed us with their guns in their hands.

When we reached the outside area I could feel the breeze off of the ocean and smell the salt in the air. I gulped down the fresh air and I looked around but could only see ocean. There were no cities or lights, just a lot of ocean, so I guess we were still offshore. I kept wondering what was happening and where was America. As we moved closer to the edge of the ship I could see two large fishing boats below.

The men motioned us to go down the ladder to the boats below. I started climbing down the ladder and when I reached the deck of the boat below another man grabbed me and pushed me towards a small doorway going down into the boat. The girls that had went before me were huddled together in a small cabin area. No one spoke, but concern and fear of what was to come hung heavy in that cabin. When the last girl was pushed into the cabin there were twelve of us. The door was closed and I could hear the man by the door talking, in English, so I didn't understand him. I heard the motors start and we were moving. We went for maybe an hour or two when I could feel the boat slow and then come to stop. The door opened and we were motioned to come out. The night air felt so good and I thought to myself, *if only Su-Lin was here to feel this.* I could hear the waves slapping against the side of the boat. Thinking about Su-Lin, my heart felt heavy with sorrow as I stepped from the boat onto a wooden dock. I could see a large house ahead of us as we walked the dock towards the beach. Another man, with a gun, was standing at the end of the dock and he motioned us toward the house. A large door was open on the side of the house and we were herded like cattle to the door and into a large room under the house.

An Asian lady was standing on a stairway that looked to go up into the house. The men motioned us to sit on the bare floor. After sitting on the floor one of the non-Asian men stepped in front of us and spoke in a language I didn't understand. He then motioned for the non-Asian girls to go into another room. They all filed into the other room as we remained seated on the floor.

The Asian lady came down the stairs, while looking at us. She looked over us and with a serious look on her face and in Chinese said, "You have completed the longest part of your journey. It's time for you to begin your new life. You are our property and you will work for us, where we put you. You owe us a great debt and you will work for us to repay it. If you make trouble you will be punished severely and if you run away or try to run away your family in Hong Kong will be punished. No one in this country will help you. You have no passport, no visa and most of you speak little or no English. Even if you manage to get away and go to the authorities you will be treated as a criminal in this country and punished severely."

She circled us while looking at each one of us, "In a moment you will be allowed to take a hot shower, receive new clothes and will be fed a good meal. Just remember, don't screw with me or you'll regret it."

She turned saying something to one of the men in English and left up the stairs into the house.

One of the men stood watching us as we were told to undress and go into the shower. I tried to hide my body with my hands as much as possible. But as I stood under the hot water my inhibitions left me. It was so good to wash the grime, sweat and the smell of death from my body. I didn't even think about the man watching me. Stepping out of the shower, I was handed a large towel and motioned to the side. A pile of clothes were folded neatly on a table in front of a mirror. I began to dress in a nice pair of pants and a sweatshirt with English writing on the front of it. I picked up a hairbrush off the table and began to brush my long coal black hair, as I stood in front of the mirror. As I stood there, I could see an image of Mom behind me, brushing my hair as she had always done. Then I came back from my memories and she wasn't there.  They brought us rice with vegetables and meat to eat.  We washed it down with hot tea.  It was happily accepted after what we had to eat on the ship for so many days.  They brought us bedrolls.  Then they turned the lights down low and told us to sleep.

The *fog is so thick.  Bright lights moving in front of me.  An image in the fog, no, two images in the fog. I can't see them clearly.  Someone is talking, I can't understand them.  I try to speak but nothing comes out.  I try to raise my hand and touch one of the images, my hand won't move.  The lights and the images are moving away from me. Now it grows darker, darker and so quite.  I try to yell out, No, No, please don't go. But I am consumed in darkness and silence.*

Chapter 5

When I awoke the next morning, other than the sadness in my heart from losing Su-Lin

and the fear of what lay ahead for me, I felt a little better.  The hot shower and meal made me

almost feel like more than some sort of lowly animal.  The non-Asian girls never returned during

the night.  I didn't know if they were in another room or had been taken from the house.  That

left seven of us Asians in the room.  Then I remembered the little bible Su-Lin had gave me. I

looked around the room for my old clothes but they were gone and so was the bible.  My heart

dropped to my stomach and tears came to my eyes as I thought of Su-Lin giving me the bible

and me saying the prayer on the ship.  How was I going to keep Jesus close to me without the

bible?  As my eyes swelled with tears I wondered if he would ignore me or not want me since I

had lost the bible.

The Asian lady and one of the men came down the stairs after we had been fed a hot

breakfast.  They opened a closet door off to our side and rolled out a television on a cart in

front of us.  As the man was plugging it in and preparing it the lady stood in front of us.

She said, "We are going to show you some movies and you'll watch them. If I see you looking away or closing your eyes you'll be punished. You will learn from them what you will be expected to do in order to perform the work we require of you."

As the movie started to play I wanted to turn away from it but didn't for fear of being punished. There was a man and a woman on the film doing all sorts of bad things to each other. They were doing things that I had never heard of and I knew I could never do. I instinctively closed my eyes to block it out but was slapped very hard in the back of the head by the man in the room. I opened my eyes and continued watching but I kept thinking, *I'll never do this.*

We were forced to watch the movies over and over through the day. The only time we weren't watching was when they brought us our food for lunch. After lunch we continued watching the movies. At the end of the day the lady looked at us and said, "Any questions of what is required?"

The girl sitting next to me yelled at her, "I won't do that stuff, I want to go home!"

The lady motioned to the man and he immediately grabbed the girl by the hair and pulled her off to the side of our little group. He began to slap her and was tearing her clothes off. She was screaming and trying to fight back, but it was to no avail. As I shook and cried from the horror of what was happening, he raped her in front of us. She lay on the floor crying as the man straightened his clothes and stood over her.

The lady stared at us and with a stern voice said, "This is what can happen if you give me a hard time and believe me, a lot worst things can be done to you! Don't give us any crap and you'll have no problems." Her voice became soft and she smiled saying, "Who knows you may like it."

She motioned to the girl laying on the floor and said to us, "Clean her up and put new clothes on her." Then she went up the stairs with the man and closed the door behind her.

As we helped the girl to the shower and helped her clean herself, she said nothing, but just hung her head in shame and cried. No one said anything to her, but helped her shower and put on new clothes. I picked up the hair brush and brushed her hair in silence.

For two days after that we were required to look at the videos. We all watched the videos and there were no further outburst from any of us for fear of severe punishment or the same horrible thing that the other girl had experienced. I felt like I was in a nightmare and kept hoping I would wake up and be back home in Mom's arms, but I knew this was for real. The girl that was raped watched the movies with tears in her eyes and flowing down her face.

*I can barely see an image of a face in front of me. The fog is so thick. I see a bright light moving back and forth in front of me. The image is talking to me, but I don't understand. I try to touch the face with my hand, but I can't move. I try to talk, but nothing comes out. Where am I? Who are you? What is happening to me? I want to say, please help me, help me, but nothing comes out. The lights and the image start to move away from me. Oh no, it's getting dark again. No, please don't go, please don't go. Please help me. But it grows darker, darker, and darker and I am consumed in darkness and silence.*

The door to the outside opened and the lady and two men came into the room. They motioned us to come. We were led to a large van, with no windows or seats in the back of it.

They pushed us into the van and slammed the door shut. I could see the Asian lady standing in front of the van talking to the men. The lady turned and went back into the house. The men climbed into the front of the van and we started moving. We rode for a long time in the van, only stopping once at a park of some sort as it was getting dark. It gave us a chance to stretch our legs and move around. They had a cooler full of water and gave each of us a bottle of water. We were there for quite a bit as it started to grow darker outside. One of the men told us to get back in the van. He said we had about two more hours to our destination. Where we had stopped was in the country and it was next to a really big highway. There were no cities or people to be seen. The only thing we seen were lots of cars and trucks going by on the highway. One of the girls had noticed a large sign on the highway but she only knew the alphabet. She said it had the letters *okl* on it but was unable to see more. Sitting in the floor of the van and with no windows in the back we were unable to see anything. We stretched out as best we could in the van. The girl that sit next to me was the one that had been raped. Her name was Ah Lam and she was thirteen. She had not spoken even one word since that horrible day. She seemed to walk around in shock with a blank look on her face. If you said anything to her she would hang her head and say nothing. She had slept close to me after the incident and I could tell she had lots of bad dreams because she would scream and cry softly in her sleep.

I thought a lot about Mom and wished I was back home. I missed her so much and hoped she was okay. I worried that if I did anything to offend these people they might bring harm to her and I couldn't live with that. Sometimes I thought about Bo and Su-Lin. I didn't know if Bo would meet her in heaven because I didn't know if Bo even knew Jesus. I hoped they would meet and be good friends. I could look up to the front of the van and see it was very dark outside.  As I looked around inside the van all of the other girls were sleeping.  I leaned back against the side of the van and closed my eyes.

*The fog is all around me and is so thick.  There are lights in the fog.  I try to look at the lights and now an image of a face has appeared in front of me.  It's talking to me, but I think it's English and I can't understand what is being said.  I try to yell at them and tell them to speak Chinese, but nothing comes out.  I try to touch the face in the fog, but I can't move my arm.  Now another face has appeared and they seemed to be talking to each other.  Why can't they hear me and why can't I touch them?  What is going on?  No, no, please. The fog and the faces are moving away from me.  Please don't go, please don't go. It is growing dark, darker and now darkness and silence have consumed me.*

When I woke up the van had stopped. I tried to look out the front and see where we were but one of the men told me to sit down and don't move.  After a short time the side door of the van slid back.  An old Chinese woman looked in the van.  She stared at each of us then turned and said something to one of the men.

She looked back in the van and said, "Come, follow me.  Be quick about it.  Hurry!"

We piled out of the van, I took a quick look around and could see big buildings around us and lots of big signs with lots of lights on them.  We were behind one building in some sort of alley because there was a large trash can next to us.  We were hurried into the building.  Inside the building we were in a long dimly lit hallway with doors on each side of the hall.  I could hear music and people laughing and groaning behind some of the doors.  As we followed the old lady down the hall we were startled by a loud buzzer sounding.

36

I heard a girl call out in Chinese, "We have a customer. Is anyone available?"

Then I heard another girl call out, "Hualing, go to the front. You have a customer. Be quick about it."

The old lady opened a door along the hall and motioned us into a small room. As I was going in the door a young Chinese girl came around the corner holding the hand of an older white man. I stopped to look but one of the men that had been behind me all the way from the van pushed me into the room. They told us to sit on the floor and be quite. I don't know what the young Chinese girl had been saying to the old man. She was dressed in very short shorts and was wearing a very tight brightly colored top. It seemed to me they knew each other. The old lady came into the room with an arm full of blankets. She dropped them on the floor and left again. After a short time she came into the room with a large bowl of rice and smaller bowls for us. She passed them around the room and said she would be back, as she left the room. When she returned she had a large steaming bowl of meat and vegetables. She was followed by a younger Chinese girl carrying a box full of bottles of water. The young girl set the box on the floor and looked around at us before leaving the room.

The old lady softly said," Eat and then sleep. Do not leave this room unless one of us is with you. If you need to go to the restroom or anything let one of them know." Pointing at the two Chinese men who had been in the van with us.

There was lots of activity around us during the night. We could hear people laughing, talking, groaning and sometimes screaming. Later during the night I had to use the restroom. I told one of the men and he motioned for me to follow him. We went out the door and started down the hall with doors on both sides. At the end of the hall he opened a door that went into a small restroom. He waited outside the door as I did my business. On the way back to the room a door opened suddenly and a young scantily clad girl emerged directly into us. Before she closed the door behind her I saw a man lying nude on a bed in the room. The man behind me pushed my shoulder and told me to go on. The young girl gave us an awkward smile and went the other way. Once we were back in the room I sat on the floor with my back against the wall. I closed my eyes thinking about all that had happened. As tears flowed from the corner of my eyes I thought about Mom. I missed her so much and hoped she was okay. I thought of that horrible day when Bo died in my arms. I could see Su-Lin as she handed the bible to me and then closed her eyes and left me. I don't know what happened to the bible but it was probably thrown away with my clothes. I wasn't sure if Jesus was with me or not, without the bible. I dried my eyes and tried to sleep.

*"Mei-Lan, you need to wake up and listen to me," the voice said.*

*I opened my eyes to see Bo standing in front of me smiling down at me. I was so shocked to see him. I started to stand to hug him but he stuck his hand out in front of me as if to say stay seated.*

He said, *"Don't talk. Just listen to me. You are strong and you grew tough on the streets. Tougher than you realize. I'm sorry I am not here to protect you but you can survive. Stay tough and always be aware of what is around you. No matter what happens to you, never give up. Always look for an opportunity to overcome."*

*He motioned to my side and I turned my head in that direction. I almost screamed with joy when I saw Su-Lin standing to my side. I was in shock. She looked so beautiful as if she had never been sick.*

*She smiled at me, "Mei-Lan, stay strong. Thank you for your friendship and being there for me. Thank you for the compassion you shared with me. I want you to know that he is still with you. He will always be with you. As you walk the horrible road ahead of you and face so many hardships and struggles he will always walk with you. He has prepared a home in heaven for you. You are my sister in Christ and I will be here to receive you when it is your time."*

I jumped to my feet to embrace her but she was gone.

One of the men said, "What's wrong with you? Sit down and go back to sleep!"

It was just a dream or was it. I leaned back against the wall and closed my eyes. I knew that Jesus was still with me and I had a feeling of joy in my heart. With him I would survive. These people would not break me. I will be strong until the end, if need be. They may break or destroy my body but I will never fear, because Jesus is with me. I will be my protector with him in me.

Chapter 6


I slept well that night, after sleep finally came. I was awoken the next morning by the old lady coming into the room. She brought us a breakfast of rice and fried eggs. It went down good and I was very thankful for hot food. After we ate, one by one we were taken down the hall to the restroom. Standing in front of the restroom mirror I recognized a new person in me. Not being very experienced at prayer I bowed my head and said, "Thank you Jesus. Thank you for last night."

I left the restroom after washing my face and was escorted back to the room. After everyone had their time in the restroom we just sat on the floor in the room. The old lady came into the room and whispered something to the men. They motioned for us to get up and come into the hall. We filed out of the room and were stood along the wall next to each other. She then went to the front of the building and shortly returned with a younger woman. . The woman was very well dressed. She walked and carried herself giving the appearance of a very strong woman. As she walked up to us the men bowed very low to her and I knew she was a woman of power. She walked up to the first girl on the end of our line. She looked her over from head to toe.  She had her turn around facing the wall and looked her over again.  She then had her turn back facing her.  The lady touched the top of the girls head and ran her fingers through the girl's hair.  She asked the girl how old she was and after being told fourteen, she asked her if she had ever been with a man.  The girl said no to her and then the lady moved to the next girl in line.  It was the girl that was raped at the house.  She had the girl go through the same inspection as the first.  Before she asked her the questions one of the men stepped up to the lady and bowed. Then he whispered something to her.

After the man stepped back from her, she faced the girl and said, "How old are you?"

The girl hung her head and said, "Thirteen."

It was the first time she had talked since that night at the house.

The lady cracked an evil smile and said, "I guess you have been with a man.  Did you enjoy it?"

The girl just kept her head lowered and said nothing.

Lifting the girls head up to look ahead the lady smiled, "You had it rough the first time so from now on it will be different.  You will learn to enjoy it and enjoy the company of a man."

The lady let out a little laugh and then moved to the next girl.  It was the same as with the first girl.  When my turn came I looked her directly in the face and stood straight and tall.

She looked me in the eyes and said, "I sense no fear in you.  You're not afraid of me?"

I looked straight at her and said, "No. I'm not scared of you. I know you are a powerful lady. You could do anything to me that you desire and I can't stop you. But I'm not afraid of you or what you might do to me."

She grinned and asked, "How old are you?"

I replied, "Thirteen."

Almost before I even finished answering her question she slapped me hard, knocking me back against the wall.

She laughed again, saying, "This one will need to be broken and then she'll be good for our customers."

She then moved on to the next girls and continued with her inspection. After she finished with the last girl she stepped back from us and looked at all of us again. Passing me up she pointed at three of the girls in the line, one of which was the girl that had been raped.

"I will take them and send the usual amount in payment."

The men acknowledged what she had said and bowed to her. She then turned from us and went back to the front of the building. They then pulled the three girls from the line and the old lady motioned for them to follow her. As they walked away from us, the girl that had been raped turned and looked at me with tears in her eyes. The men then motioned us to follow down the hall and out the door we had first came in the night before. We were piled back into the van and started on another journey. No one spoke a word. We remained silent as the van started and we left from that place.

I could see the man in the passenger seat talking on a cell phone. It was light outside and I think we were in a lot of traffic because we kept stopping and then going again. After a little while we started to pick up speed and there was no more stopping. I sat back against the wall of the van and said to myself, *I was very afraid of that witch but I wasn't going to show her or let her know. I'm proud of the way I stood before her. I am a strong person.*

I thought of the night before when I had seen Bo and Su-lin. I had a warm feeling and a smile came to my face as I thought. *Bo is in a better place. He's in Heaven with my friend and sister Su-Lin.* I closed my eyes and didn't even think of what might be coming on the road ahead of me. I became very relaxed and fell to sleep with that thought in my mind.

I woke up as the van came to a stop. We must have been back in traffic because we kept going and stopping. Plus we were not moving as fast as we had earlier. I looked up towards the front of the van and just happened to see a large clock on a building as we passed it. The clock showed 2:30, so I we had been travelling for a long time. I wasn't sure but I think we had been on the road for maybe four to five hours. No one in the van was talking or had been saying anything. Even the two men in front never spoke. The three other girls with me had been silent the entire trip. After travelling for a short time more and making a lot of turns we came to a stop. The man in the passenger seat turned and told us to remain seated. He then exited from the van and the driver remained seated behind the steering wheel of the van. Shortly the side door of the van slid open. An Asian girl, maybe in her thirties, stood at the door. She looked at us and then in Chinese told us to come with her. As I climbed out the side of the van I seen a door open in front of us going into a building. Again I seen a large green trash can to our side so I think we were in a sort of alley behind a building.

We followed the girl in through the door with the two men directly behind us.  We were in another long hallway.  Again there were doors on both sides of the hall and there were numbers on each of the doors.  We came to another door with no number but English writing on it.  The girl opened the door and it was a restroom.  We took turns using the restroom and waiting in the hall until everyone was done.  After everyone was finished she motioned us into another room across the hall.  There was no furniture in the room except for a table with a TV on it and there was a large straw mat on the floor with a few pillows and blankets scattered around the room.  We were told to find a place to sit on the floor and be quite.  The two men stood just inside the door on both sides of the door.

After a short time the door opened and an older Chinese lady came into the room.  The two men both bowed to her and she bowed back to them.  She was very rough looking with a large scar on one side of her face.  Her hair, with lots of grey in it, was cut short on the sides and the back.  She wasn't dressed nice like the lady at the last place we had stopped. She was wearing an old sweatshirt and baggy pants. She looked around the room at each of us.  She walked over and stopped directly in front of me.

She looked down at me and asked, "How old are you and what are you called?"

Looking directly up at her I replied, "I'm thirteen and I am Mei-Lan."

She smiled and said, "That's a pretty name, it's a beautiful flower, an orchid."

She thought for a moment and then in English said, "Rose."

Then in Chinese she said, "That is your new name, it also is a beautiful flower and men like to be with beautiful flowers."

I wasn't sure what to think about this lady. She smiled a lot and spoke very softly as she went around the room addressing the other girls in the same manner and giving them an English name.

She turned to the men and said, "Good, they'll all be good. I'll make arraignments for payment in the usual manner. I need new blood. I have lots of customers and they are always asking about new girls. Some will pay very good money for a young virgin." She laughed and said," They'll do nicely."

She looked around the room at us again and said, "I'll have some hot food brought to you. You must be hungry. I take care of my girls."

She then left the room.

I wasn't sure how to take her. She looked very rough but was nice to all of us, almost like a mother. I looked at the other girls and they seemed to be more relaxed. I thought to myself, *she can call me 'Rose' or whatever she wants but I will always be Mei-Lan.*

It wasn't long before two girls entered the room. One was carrying a large container of rice and the other had a bowl of steaming soup with vegetables and meat mixed together. It looked good but smelled even better. Small bowels were passed to each of us, including the two men. As everyone began to eat, I almost said out loud that it was better than the scraps Mom had brought from the restaurant but I would rather be at home with mom eating the scraps.  I didn't say it, but just ate the food knowing I needed to keep my energy up for what lay ahead of me.

It wasn't long until the lady came back in the room and talked with the men.  The men bowed to her and left the room.  We never seen them again after that.

She turned to us, "You're now part of my happy little family here.  You can address me as Ms. Lee or you can call me momma.  It doesn't matter.  I think you will learn quickly that if you obey me and keep my customers happy I'll be very good to you.  But if you give me trouble or one of my customer's trouble, then you'll regret it.  Now rest.  You have had a long trip and you must be tired."

She turned and walked out of the room closing the door behind her.  I heard the lock on the door turn.  I knew then that she had said we were family, but we were prisoners.

The only time we were allowed to leave the room was when Ms. Lee came and escorted us to the restroom.  We spent the remainder of the day and that night locked in that room.

We had good meals and were able to relax.  We really didn't talk much among ourselves.  We were all still in shock of what had happened to us so far.  During the night there was lots of activity in the hall.  Voices and laughter was common.  A long time passed before anyone came to the room. When Ms. Lee finally came to the room she was accompanied by an older white man.  They talked in English and laughed.  He looked at us and smiled.  He said something to her and she patted him on the back before they left the room.

We had been in that room for a long time.  I think it was the entire night.

In the morning Ms. Lee came into the room and sat down in front of us.

She smiled again and said, "Okay, let's talk. I have rules here and you must follow those rules. I will treat you good, but if you break the rules you will be punished. I paid a lot of money to have you here and you should be thankful because you could have gone to other places that can be really horrible. There you would be treated as nothing more than a piece of meat. I have good clients here. Some have been coming here for a long time. They know my rules. They don't hurt you in any way. They'll respect you and you'll show them the utmost respect. If I lose a client because of something you do or don't do I will punish you severely. The services you'll perform for them are done every day by girls all around the world for men. It is said, it is the oldest profession in the world. I myself have worked providing services for men and learned to enjoy it. We are open seven days a week, but unlike some, we are only open certain hours. If you wake up and don't feel well or you are starting your monthly time I will excuse you from work. As I said, I'll be good to you. There are three other girls here and they have been working very hard. It is good you're here and this is your home now and we are the only family you will have. Do as your told, make no trouble and life will be good for you. Any questions? You will begin today by cleaning and washing the rooms. I have washing machines and lots of sheets and towels that need washing on a daily basis. For a few days that will be your responsibilities. You'll help with those jobs and also help fix food for your family. Okay, Come with me."

She led us out of the room towards the back of the building down the hallway to another door. She opened the door and motioned us in. It was a large room with a washer and dryer on one side. There was a table in the middle and a rack on the other side with lots of bottles of liquids on it. She opened the door of the dryer and pulled a bundle of sheets from it and tossed them on the table. She then opened the washer and pulled the towels out and threw them in the dryer. We spent the day learning how to operate the machines and the uses of the various bottles of liquids in the rack. She pointed out where the dirty sheets and towels were tossed. She took us to one of the rooms off of the hallway. It was small and there was a table or more like a bed in the center of the room with enough room to walk around it. There was a small table in one corner with small bottles of liquids on it and a small CD player, with a clock. The table had a soft top on it and was covered with a sheet. Underneath the table was a shelf with folded clean sheets and towels on it.

She walked around the table and said, "This a massage room and where you'll perform your job later. Some of our clients only want a relaxing massage but some, most want more."

She pointed at the table, "Those are lotions that are used during the massage. And that CD player is used to provide relaxing music for the client during the massage. Tonight after dinner you will start watching movies to learn proper massage techniques that will make the client feel good. You will be taught all you need to know. And as I said, some of our customers want more. For a price we give them what they want. You will be taught what to do in order to please the customer. For a while you will just be cleaning and doing other duties before you are ready for a customer. If you just do what is expected of you then all will be good."

She motioned us out of the room and back to what she called the laundry room. She showed us how she wanted the towels and sheets folded. She then assigned each of us different jobs and told us to get to work.

Chapter 7

*The fog is thick.  I can see into the fog and see an image of a face with bright lights around it.  They're talking to me, not in Chinese.  I don't understand what's being said.  I can hear them very plain, but just don't understand.  I want to tell them to speak Chinese, but nothing comes out.  I try to touch the face in the fog, but can't move my hand.  Why am I unable to move or talk?  Where am I?  Who are these people I keep seeing in the fog? What's happening to me? The fog is turning dark and the face is moving away from me.  I don't hear them now.  I am consumed in darkness and silence around me.*

We spent the day cleaning and doing laundry.  I learned that there were eight of the rooms with massage tables in them.  They were all set up the same way.  During the day a lot of men were escorted from the front, by one of the other three girls, to different massage rooms. The men were of all different races.  Some were white and others were black.  Sometimes they would smile at me as we passed in the hall.  The girls seemed to be very busy with a constant flow of men throughout the day.

Ms. Lee came through the hall every so often checking on us.  Finally, after a long day, she came and took us back to the room where we had slept the night before.  An older Chinese lady that we had not seen before brought our food to us.  Ms. Lee came after we had eaten and pulled the table with the TV on it into the center of the room.  She turned it on and put a DVD in the player.

She said," Watch this movie and you'll begin to learn how to give a massage.  This is important because this will be a big part of your job in order to please your client.  Don't let me catch you sleeping.  Just watch the movie and learn."  She then turned and left the room.  I heard the lock turn in the door.

I leaned back against the wall and watched the movie.  We were starting to talk more amongst ourselves.  We had learned each other's name and about the promises we had been made, before coming to America.  We all new that we had been lied to and we were not going to see the pretty house or live with the American family.  We sat watching the massage video and talked about what we were seeing. We all agreed that if that was all we had to do it wouldn't be so bad.  I didn't say anything to them or question them about what they wanted to do.  But I knew that all I wanted was to get back to mom and put this behind me.  If I had an opportunity to do it, I would.

We spent the next few days cleaning and washing towels and sheets.  Sometimes we were taken to the front of the building to clean.  There was a small window with a door next to it that led into another room.  There was a small sofa and a table that had magazines on it in the room.  It was a waiting room for the customers.  We were always under the watchful eye of Ms. Lee when we were in this area.  There were no windows in the room but the door going outside was glass.  I could see a busy street with lots of traffic passing by.  One day while cleaning that area a well-dressed white man came in the door from the street.  Ms. Lee greeted him when he came in and he returned the greeting.  He went to the window and pushed a button on the wall next to it.  I heard music, which I think was activated by him pushing the button.  One of the girls, that was already there when we had come, opened the window.  They talked and then he took money from his pocket and handed it to her.  The door opened and she let him in, smiling and talking the whole time.

At times during the day we were led back to our room and watched videos on massage and also videos teaching basic greetings and phrases in English.   We had been there for a few days before we were introduced to the other girls.  As we would pass in the hall they would greet me in English with phrases such as, *Good morning Rose or Hello Rose.*

One afternoon Ms. Lee collected us together and took us to the front.  She opened a door on the side of the hall next to the window and motioned us in.  It was a larger room with a large TV on the wall, a refrigerator along the wall, a cooking stove next to the refrigerator and shelves on the wall containing bowels, cans of food and other assorted items.  There was no other furniture in the room but there were bedrolls that were rolled up and lying next to the wall.  There was another door that went into a bathroom area that also had a shower in it.

Ms. Lee faced us and said, "Go collect your bedrolls from the other room and bring them here.  This is where you'll now stay.  You'll be here with us.  You'll now start to learn some of the daily duties other than cleaning. Go, be quick about it and hurry back."

I retrieved my bedroll and laid it along the wall in the new room.  Only one girl was in the room. The other two were with customers.  Ms. Lee started showing us how to operate the stove and how to prepare the meals.  I noticed a big round clock on the wall in the room.  I had

51

learned to tell time in Hong Kong and it showed 6:30 and I knew it was probably in the evening. While we were helping Ms. Lee prepare the meal, music from the front door button started to play. The girl went out the door to the small window. I think it was a customer because she didn't come back for a little as she was probably escorting him to one of the rooms. When she came back she handed Ms. Lee some money and then left again.

After a few days more had passed I was walking down the hall taking clean sheets to one of the rooms. Ms. Lee was standing in the hall talking to a nice looking white man. He wasn't old, but not young either. I guess he was middle age. As I passed, he smiled at me and in English said, "Hello Rose."

I returned his smile and replied in English, "Hello and Good Morning."

As I went into the room with the sheets I seen him, out of the corner of my eye, counting out a lot of money to Ms. Lee. When I came out of the room he was gone and Ms. Lee was walking in the hall towards me.

She smiled, "Rose, come with me. You have your first customer."

My pulse started to race and I wanted to run away but where would I go?

She looked at me and grabbed my hand, "Come, come it will be okay."

We went into our living area and she grabbed a wet rag and started washing my face then she had a hairbrush and started brushing my long black hair.

As she brushed my hair she spoke, "All you have to do is just give him a good massage as you have seen on the videos. It doesn't have to be perfect. He is a nice man and a regular that spends a lot of money here. He knows it's your first time. So don't worry. You'll be fine."

She led me down the hall to the room he occupied. I was so nervous and scared that I was shaking all over. My stomach felt like it was tied in knots. He was lying nude on his stomach as we entered the room. He rolled over slightly showing all of his nudity, to say hello. He continued smiling at me as Ms. Lee spoke to him in English and then she turned and left closing the door behind her.

My legs were shaking as I walked to the side of the table. With trembling hands and sweat running down my face I began to rub his back. He dropped his hand to the side of the table and began to rub the back of my legs. I stepped back and moved to the front of the table by his head. I started massaging his neck as I had seen on the video. He brought his hands up behind me and started caressing my backside. I trembled all over and felt sick. I pulled away from him and started for the door. He quickly sat up on the table, grabbing me by the hair as I passed. He pulled me back to him, suddenly slipping one arm around my waist pulling me tight against him as his other hand went up inside my shirt groping my chest. In disbelief and horror I started jabbing my elbows back into him attempting to break free. He was to strong and picked me up with the arm around my waist. Swinging around, he threw me on the table. I closed my eyes while trying to strike him in the face with my fist. He held me down with one hand around my throat and the other up my shirt. As he squeezed harder around my throat I could feel things going black. I panicked even more when I thought, he was going to choke me to death. I tried to fight harder but it was useless. I felt myself losing consciousness.

*The fog is now so thick that it's hard to breath. I can't breathe. I can see the image of a face in the fog. I yell for them to help me, I can't breathe. Please help me! I don't want to die. Please help me! They are talking to me but not in Chinese. I don't understand. I want to reach up and grab them, but my arms won't move. I try to yell for help, but nothing comes out. No, oh no, they are leaving me to die. Please don't go. It's getting dark again and I don't hear anything now. Only silence and darkness surround me.*

I felt something cold on my face and slowly started to open my eyes. Ms. Lee was standing at the edge of the table, wiping my face with a wet rag.

Realizing what had happened to me, my eyes started to swell with tears. I could feel that my clothes were gone. I had been violated. He raped me.

Ms. Lee covered me with a sheet while saying, "You're okay now. It's all over now. You are no longer a child. You're now a woman."

I looked at her and rage filled my heart. I wanted to kill her and that man. She knew what was going to happen. She knew what he was going to do to me. He had paid her for that. I wanted both of them dead.

My body trembled as she helped me off the table and with a sheet around me, led me down the hall. I felt my legs were going to collapse and my feet wouldn't move. As I entered our living area the other three new girls were sitting along the wall. I pulled the sheet up over my head, not wanting them to see me, as Ms. Lee led me to the shower. My stomach could not take the knots in it any longer and I let it go, puking all over the bathroom floor. She turned the water on and put me under the water from the shower. I heard her yell at the other girls to come and clean up the mess. I stood under the hot water with a bar of soap in my hands. I began to scrub my body as hard as I could with the soap and a rag. I had to wash the shame and the scent of the man from my body. I scrubbed and scrubbed with the rag as hard as I could. I leaned my head against the wall of the shower and cried. I wished he had killed me.

The voice was soft, but firm, *"You have nothing to be ashamed of. You did nothing to be ashamed of, they did it. They are trying to break you, not kill you. Don't let them. Be strong. He's not ashamed of you. You are his child and he loves you. Stay strong in faith. You are stronger than these people. It is written, you can do all things through him."*

I sat in the floor of the shower as the water ran over my body. My strength started to return. I said to myself, *"I am strong and will not be broken. I will overcome. Thank you Jesus."*

I grabbed a towel and dried off. As I walked out of the bathroom one of the other girls handed me clean clothes and asked, "Are you okay?"

With a strong voice I replied, "I'll be okay. Thank you."

I stared straight at Ms. Lee as she stood by the stove fixing a meal. She caught my stare and quickly looked away from me.

I looked at the other three girls sitting along the wall. I could see the fear for what had happened to me in their eyes, they knew their time would come. As I looked at them I made myself a promise. One way or the other I would escape from this life and I would take them with me. Through his strength I knew that I could do it. I don't know how or when but it will come about. I will overcome.

Customers kept coming as usual but Ms. Lee let me be for a few days. I kept busy washing clothes and cleaning. During that time the other girls were introduced to various men. When they came back from the ordeal I was there for them. I helped them to shower and gave them a shoulder to cry on. I wanted to tell them about Jesus but wasn't sure what to say.

One day Ms. Lee collected us all together and took us into the laundry room. She stood in front of us, "You're all young women now. You have been with a man. Whether you enjoyed it or not matters not to me. You will start receiving customers now. It is time for you to start working to repay your debt to me. We will be very selective about your customers. I tell you again as before. If you are bad or don't please a customer you will be punished. And I promise there are a lot worst things can happen to you than what you have experienced thus far. Accept it, because if not, I will sell you to a lower establishment. You are all under age so I have special precautions to protect you. I we're ever busted, they will put you in hard labor camps and you won't last more than a few months."

She walked to the shelf with the bottles of liquids on it. She grabbed it and pulled hard. To my shock, it moved away from the wall and revealed a sliding door behind it. She slid the door open and walked into a very small room, not even as big as the bathroom in our living area. The room was empty of furniture or anything else. It was just a cement floor and walls. Ms. Lee pointed in the room and said, "If we are going to be raided you'll go into this room, pull the shelf back to the wall and close the door. Be quite and don't move until myself or one of the older girls come and tell you it is all clear. Do you understand?"

We all nodded in unison to understanding what she had said.

Pointing at the dirty sheets and the machines she said, "Now get to work. You have work to do."

As I was folding sheets on the table one of the older girls entered the room with dirty sheets from her last customer. She was called Candy and I knew she was about twenty-two years old. The other three girls, my age, were cleaning rooms.

I greeted her and asked, "How long have you been here?"

She began helping men fold the sheets, "Almost five years, Ms. Lee bought me from another place where I had been working for over a year."

"Candy, why do you do this?"

She lowered her head, "What can I do? I have no passport. I'm illegal in this country. If I did leave, where would I go? If I don't work hard here she will sell me to another place. And trust me, this is a world better than other places that might buy you. Some of them drug you and you don't do massages but are just used by men for sex all the time, maybe fifteen or twenty times in a day. You are just a piece of meat that they make money from. Also, do you have family back home?"

"Yes, my Mom is in Hong Kong."

"Well, they would make life hell for her and maybe even hurt or torture her. And I promise you, they would be sure to show you pictures or videos of it. Would you want that to happen? I don't think so."

"No, I couldn't live with that."

57

"Then just don't rock the boat. Do what Ms. Lee tells you. Please your customers, even though you may hate what you are doing. You won't have as many customers as me and the other older girls. She can get a lot more money for you guys than us. They pay big for young girls. Hell, I bet she got two or three thousand for you from that first guy. He paid dearly to be your first and be the one to deflower you."

We heard Ms. Lee calling, "Candy, where are you? Get up front, you have a customer."

Candy gave me a serious look, "Remember, don't rock the boat. And don't piss her off."

As she left the room, I thought about all she had said. I really didn't worry about me so much as I did what they might do to Mom.

Every day, Ms. Lee would have us sit and watch more massage movies and sex movies. Sometimes she would have us practice massage on each other. I really didn't have a problem doing the massage. It was the other things a customer might want that bothered me.

A few days later I had my next customer. Ms. Lee escorted him to the room and then took me to the room. She introduced me to him and then left. He was old and his hair was solid white. He was small, not very tall, and was very thin. His skin was very pale and wrinkled. He lay nude on the table and kept telling me I was very pretty.

Thinking about what had happened to me before, I stepped close to the table with caution. With my hands shaking and sweat on my forehead I began to massage his back as hard as I could and then began working my way down to his feet. He didn't say anything but just laid there. After working on his feet, I moved to the front of the table and began a slow massage to the back of his neck. I was thankful that he hadn't moved or tried rubbing me like the first man had done. While massaging his neck I noticed, I couldn't hear him breathing. I jumped back from the table, oh, my God, he was dead. I stepped back against the wall, staring at him, not knowing what I should do. My body started to tremble and my hands were shaking uncontrollably. What would Ms. Lee do to me if I had killed a customer? I started to move towards the door when I heard it. He was snoring, he was asleep. I was so overcome with relief and joy that I started to cry and then softly laughed.

I leaned back against the wall and watched him as he slept. I took one large towel and covered his backside then stood there and waited. I kept watching the little timer that was on the table. When his hour was almost up I stepped to the front of the table, by his head, and began massaging his scalp with slow, soft strokes. He began to stir from sleep and move around. I patted him on the back as he sat up on the table. He stood and stretched while reaching for his pants. Pulling a twenty dollar bill from the pocket, he presented it to me.

He smiled and said, "Wow, thank you. That was a great massage. I really enjoyed that. That twenty is a tip for you. You did great."

I said in English, "Thank you, "while helping him put on his pants and then his shirt and shoes.

We left the room together and ran into Ms. Lee coming down the hall.

In front of her, he hugged me and said to her, "You got you a good one here. Worth every penny. I'll be back."

I wasn't exactly sure what he said but I understood enough to know it pleased Ms. Lee, who smiled and said "thank you'" to him.

We escorted him to the front and out the door.

Ms. Lee smiled at me and said, "See, that wasn't so bad was it." Then she turned and walked down the hall.

I pulled the twenty out of my pocket and thought of someplace to hide it. I didn't want anyone to know about it because I might have a need for it someday. I went back to the massage room and pulled the sheets off the table and picked up the dirty towel. After putting new sheets on the table I took the dirty linen to the laundry room. I threw the dirty linen in the hamper, all the time thinking about where would be a good hiding place for my money. I noticed a vent grill, on the bottom of a wall, on one side of the room. It had small knobs on the top and bottom. I turned the knobs and was able to pull the grill away from the wall. It was just a small empty area behind the vent grill. I think it was a sort of air vent that was no longer used. I grabbed a small towel and wrapped it around the twenty, placing it as far back, out of sight, as possible in the vent.

I was very happy with myself and how my day had gone, so far, as I left the laundry room and walked to the living area with a smile on my face.

# Chapter 8

The next day Ms. Lee collected me from the laundry room and escorted me to one of the massage rooms. She opened the door and motioned me inside. Laying on the table was a young white man. He sat up on the table exposing his nudity and smiled at me. Ms. Lee told me that he was a police detective and was a very special friend, with special benefits. He was maybe six feet tall and in pretty good shape. He looked like someone that worked out often. She said something to him in English that I didn't understand. I was getting better at my English but still had a limited vocabulary.

She moved me closer to him and he reached out and took my hand, "Hello Rose, my name's John."

I replied back with a shaky voice, "Hello."

She patted him on the back and said something to him and he responded to her with a laugh.

She looked directly at me and in Chinese said, "Be good to him and do whatever he wants or he will let me know. If you don't make him happy, you'll be very unhappy."

She turned and left the room, closing the door behind her.

He grabbed my shoulders and pulled me close to him.  He began to remove my clothes, all the time kissing me on my neck.   He stood up and then laid me down on the table.  He started to kiss me over my body.  I didn't resist in any way.  I knew it would be foolish to try to run away.  I let him do what he wanted.  I picked a point on the ceiling and stared at it trying to block out what was happening to me.

*The face was directly in front of me.  I can't see it clearly for the fog that engulfs it.  It's talking to me, but I can't understand it. I want, so much, to know who it is and what is being said.  I want to touch it with my hand but can't move.  I want to ask, where am I?  Who are you? Why can't I move?  Why can't I talk?  The fog is getting heavier or maybe the face is withdrawing deeper into the fog.  It's getting dark and I can't see the face. It's growing darker and darker until I'm again consumed in darkness and silence.*

I looked from the point and he was standing, getting dressed, next to me.  He kissed my forehead and handed me a twenty dollar bill saying, "Thank you, Rose."

I forced a smile at him as he left the room.  I immediately jumped off the table and pulled my clothes on.  I stuffed the twenty in my bra and then pulled the sheets off the table replacing them with clean ones.  When I walked from the room, Ms. Lee and him were standing together and talking by the front door.  Ms. Lee threw a glance to me and smiled as if to say, Good job.  I immediately went to the laundry room, looking back down the hall to be sure no one was behind me.  I threw the sheets in the hamper and moving as fast as possible removed the towel from behind the air vent.  I placed the twenty with the other twenty rolled up in the

towel then replaced it back in my hiding place.

I pulled sheets from the dryer and tossed them on the table, then moved the towels

from the washer to the dryer.  One of the older girls, her name Cherry, came into the laundry

room.  She tossed a handful of sheets and towels into the hamper saying, "Ms. Lee wants you in

room four."

As I entered the room she was talking to and older man.  He looked at me and smiled.

Ms. Lee said, "You have another customer.  Treat him good."

She left the room and it was a repeat of before.  He wanted me to touch him all over his

body before he laid me on my back.  As he hovered over me, I again found a point on the ceiling

and focused on it, blocking out what was going to happen to me.

From that day on, I and the other three younger girls were averaging about three

customers every day. The older girls were averaging six to seven each day.  Not everyone gave

me a tip but when they did I hid it with my little stash inside the air vent.

As time went on, I didn't think much about Jesus.  I became numb to the men that I was

with on a daily basis.  Ms. Lee seemed to be very pleased with the way things were going.  Why

not, she was making money.  We kept busy between customers working in the laundry room,

cleaning massage rooms and watching videos on English, massage and sex.

One night as I was fixing supper I heard loud screaming from the back.  Ms. Lee jumped

to her feet and started running to one of the massage rooms.  She busted into the massage room and I could hear her screaming and yelling in Chinese. She backed out of the room, dragging one of the younger girls, named Suzy, by the hair across the floor. I saw a different side of Ms. Lee I had not seen before. She began to beat and kick the girl violently while yelling obscenities at her. She dragged her down the hall into the room where we had first stayed on arriving here. I could hear the beating continue until Ms. Lee came from the room, closing and locking the door, leaving Suzy in the room. She then ran back to the massage room. I heard her yell for Candy to bring the first aid kit. I slipped back into the living area, wanting to know what had happened, but was too frightened to ask. After a short time, Candy came into the living area.

I asked, "What happened?"

She shook her head side to side and said, "She bit the customer and you don't want to know where. Ms. Lee is really pissed. No telling what she will do to her." Then she turned and went back to assist Ms. Lee.

I could hear Ms. Lee at the exit door telling the customer how sorry she was for what had happened. After the customer left she came into the living area. She was really mad. Her face was red and sweat poured down her face  Breathing hard, gritting her teeth, she said nothing but walked to a small closet and retrieved a stick, maybe an inch thick and two feet long. She went back to the room where Suzy was locked up. I could hear Ms. Lee yelling obscenities at her as she beat her with the stick.

After a long time Ms. Lee came back into the living area. Blood covered her hands and face. Sweat and blood had soaked her clothes. Not a word was said as she marched into the bathroom and closed the door.

I saw nothing else of Suzy until the next night. She never came from the room and Ms. Lee never went to the room. I was taking sheets to the laundry room after another customer and seen Ms. Lee opening the back door to the alley. A Chinese man and lady came in, closing the door behind them. They walked, with Ms. Lee, straight to the room holding Suzy. When they came from the room, the man was carrying Suzy. She was covered with bruises and blood from the beating. She opened her eyes, stared at me, and then closed them again. The man and the woman went out the door with Suzy. Ms. Lee closed the door and started walking back up the hall.

As she passed me, she stopped and stared straight at me, "Don't break the rules or piss me off." And then walked back to the front.

I never saw Suzy again. I overheard one of the older girls say, "They took her to one of the brothels." Shaking her head she said, "Cheap meat. They'll dope her up and make her available to scum, for their pleasure. She won't even know what is being done to her or by whom is doing it. They'll give her enough food to keep her alive but when no one wants her and she brings in no profit. Then they just give her to the rats and cats at the dump."

Not a word was said by any of us about the incident for fear of pissing off Ms. Lee.

Things continued as before. After a few days Ms. Lee seemed to settle back into the person I had known before. I was getting customers every day and on some days I would have four or five.  Sometimes they were repeat customers that I had been with before.  I had learned to block out the situations as they occurred.  I made myself numb to the men that took pleasure from my body.  However, many a night as I lay on my bedroll after closing and everyone was asleep I would cry quietly and think about Mom, Bo and Su-Lin.  I kept telling myself to stay strong and always be aware of any opportunity to escape from this life.  I had learned, from listening to the older girls talk, that we were a part of a large network of massage parlors and brothels all over America.  It was so hard for me to understand how this could be tolerated in a land as great as America.  Also due to the fact that a few of my customers were police officers, I knew there would be no help from the American authorities.  No one cared about us or what might happen to us.  The only way to escape was to gain their trust and maybe someday become a mamasan, like Ms. Lee, and over see one of the establishments in the network.   But I also realized that I was more likely to be killed and thrown away when ones usefulness no longer existed.  I had built up my hidden stash to over three hundred dollars, due to customer tips, and was happy about that.  I had never had that much money in my life.

I'm not sure how long I had been a prisoner in these walls.  Maybe two or three months had passed.  On one occasion I was cleaning the front lobby area under the watchful eye of Ms. Lee.  When she was called to the phone I took a quick peak out the front glass door.  A four lane street went in front of us and there was a large parking area between us and another business on one side.  I was surprised to see a number of Asian people walking along the sidewalk between us and the street.  Across the street was another business with Chinese writing on the windows. But not knowing how to read, I had no idea of what it said.  I heard the door to the hall open and Ms. Lee was saying something to one of the other girls. I let the glass door close and started cleaning it.

Over time I learned from Candy that a customer paid about two hundred dollars for our services. In most cases they paid around three hundred to spend an hour with one of us younger girls. At twenty to thirty customers a day Ms. Lee was making a lot of money.

My English got better and better. I could do greetings, *thank you, have a good day* and many other phrases. I learned what a customer was wanting by things they would say to me and I knew I had to provide those services or suffer the consequences. I was working in the laundry room when one of the other girls came and told me that Ms. Lee needed me up front.

Walking into the living area I saw a very well dressed Chinese man. He immediately walked over to me and grasped my hand gently and in English said, "Hello Rose or Mei-Lan, if you prefer. Very nice to meet you and how are you?"

In English I replied, "I'm very well and you?"

He laughed and turned to Ms. Lee speaking Chinese, "Good. She'll be perfect."

Turning his attention back to me and in Chinese said, "How old are you Mei-Lan?"

I replied, "Thirteen, almost fourteen."

"Perfect. Ms. Lee has graciously offered your services to me for a few days. I have some clients that want to spend time with younger girls. However, they will not come to establishments such as this, so you must go them. As long as you make my customers happy then I'm happy. Ms. Lee tells me that you have made no trouble here and she has received

67

some nice comments from customers concerning you. I like that. When I don't have work, you may return here."

He walked over and stood directly in front of Ms. Lee and they talked in private. I saw her nod in agreement and he then turned back to me saying, "Okay, come. You'll go with me for a few days then come back to here."

I followed him out the door into the hallway. He opened the door to the front lobby and I followed him into the lobby. As he went out the front door I hesitated. Having never been through that door I felt excitement and fear at the same time. Another Chinese man was standing next to a long, shiny black car. He opened the back door for us and bowed to the man with me. I was in awe as I climbed into the back of the car. I had never seen anything that beautiful, inside and out, before. A Chinese girl, maybe Candy's age, was already sitting in the back of the car. She smiled and greeted me as I moved across the big leather seat to the other side. Before entering the car he stood, for a moment, talking to the other man then climbed in and sat next to the girl.

"Mei-Lan, no, Rose. I'm Henry and this is Honey. She will help you with things such as clothes, makeup and that sort of thing. We are going to make a stop and do a little shopping. You need some nice clothes and other things for the work you will be performing for me. My clients are very wealthy so you must look your best."

It was already dark outside and the windows were so dark on the car I could see nothing as we went along. We came to a stop and the same man opened the door for us. Honey climbed out of the car motioning for me to follow. Henry remained seated in the car talking on a cell phone.  We had stopped in front of a large store with large windows containing mannequins that were dressed with very fancy clothes.  As Honey and I walked through the store I was in awe at all the beautiful clothes.  She picked out a number of clothes and had me try them on and model for her.  Some of the clothes were very fancy, such as a model might wear and others gave me the appearance of being a young schoolgirl.  I was so ecstatic over the beautiful clothes, shoes and jewelry she picked out for me that I forgot about where I was and what I would be doing.  After the cashier rang up the purchase, Honey produced a large quantity of one hundred dollar bills.  Pulling quite a few from the stack she handed them to the cashier.  Henry was still talking on the phone when we climbed back into the car.

Driving for quite a while, we finally stopped.  We were in front of a very large building with lots of different colored lights across the front of it.  Rows of flowers were lined up along the front of the building.  I followed Henry and Honey into the building with the other man behind us carrying the packages containing the clothes.  We entered an elevator and I saw Honey push the number ten on the panel.  As we started moving I grasped one of the rails attached to the wall.  I had never ridden in an elevator before so I was a little nervous.  We exited the elevator and walked straight to a door across from the elevator and entered it.

It was the most beautiful place I had ever seen.  It was filled with beautiful chairs and tables.  A very pretty Chinese girl was sitting in one of the chairs.  She stood and walked over to the man carrying the packages and took them from him.  She carried them into another room and then returned.

She walked up to me and in Chinese, "Hi sweetie. I'm Merci. Welcome to our little palace. You hungry?"

I shook my head to say no and she shrugged her shoulders and returned to her chair. The man that carried the packages removed his jacket revealing a gun strapped to his side, under his arm. Honey motioned for me to sit, so I sat in a large chair close to me.

Henry took a seat across from Honey and in Chinese, "I have two customers coming in tomorrow. One early in the afternoon and the other tomorrow night. You need to get her cleaned up and dressed to kill for the two appointments. The judge, tomorrow night, may want her the next day again, if he likes her. Put her in the shower and then put her to bed."

Honey told me to follow her. She led me into a large room with a big bed and lots of beautiful furniture in the room. I had never seen anything like it or the shower that she led me too next. I took a hot shower and then laid down in the bed. When Honey left the room I kept having thoughts of everything that happened. I thought, even though, I didn't like what I had to do, I did like it here. I had never slept in a bed and felt very uncomfortable. I pulled the blanket and pillow from the bed and spread them out on the floor. It didn't take me long to drift off into a heavy sleep. I don't remember the dreams that came to me that night. I think they were about the big yellow house with flowers around it.

When I awoke the next morning I put the blanket and pillow back on the bed. I walked over to a large curtain and pulled it back. It exposed a large window looking out over the city. There was a large park across the street. There was a big water fountain in the park that was surrounded by gardens containing all sorts of beautiful flowers. It reminded me of the gardens and parks in Hong Kong.  I thought back to the days Bo and I would sit in the park and munch on the fruits I was able to steal from the street vendors.  My heart was heavy with sorrow as I thought about those days and Bo.

I was startled as Honey came into the room saying, "Good, you're up.  Come and eat.  You have a busy day."

I followed her like a little puppy back into the room with the chairs.  To the side was a large table and there were bowls filled with rice and other things on the table.

She said, "Sit down and eat. After breakfast we will start on coaching you and getting you ready for this afternoon.  You are a very lucky girl that Henry picked you.  You will find life much better here.  I've been here for over a year and he treats me good.  Don't forget you are his property and never cross him or it could really go bad for you.  I would lot rather be here than some of the other establishments.  You are young, so you are a desired commodity. His clients pay big, big money for that.  Tonight you will meet the judge.  He's really a judge and has lots of power in this city.  He's a very powerful man."  She laughed and then said, "He has a weakness for young kids and Henry feeds that weakness.  Now eat."

I asked, "I thought I was going somewhere this afternoon also?"

Without looking at me she said, "Nope, that one has been cancelled."

I dug into the rice in front of me.  There was a plate of fried eggs and veggies also on the table and it was so, so tasty.  I washed it down with a large glass of orange juice and then started working on a cup of hot tea. I looked around the room and there was no one else present. Only myself and honey.

Finishing breakfast, Honey started coaching me on things to say and how to act. The judge apparently really liked very young girls. She said he would really like my long hair.

She asked, "How much English do you know."

I just shrugged my shoulders.

In English she said, "Hello. How are you?"

I replied with a big smile on my face, "I'm well. Thank you and you?"

In English, "How old are you?"

I replied, "Thirteen."

She said, "What if he says in English, You're very pretty. How will you reply?"

I said, "Thank you sir."

"No, don't say sir. Say, thank you, daddy. He'll love that."

I repeated, "Thank you, Daddy."

"Good, you have learned much English with Ms. Lee. You'll do fine and I think he'll really like you. If he likes you, then Henry will love you."

We spent the morning practicing phrases he might say and how I should reply. I became lost in what we were doing. Never once did I think about what would happen to me when we were together. I liked Honey. She was so nice and treated me as if I was her little sister.

72

We talked a lot that morning. She told me that she and Merci also had regular customers that were arraigned by Henry. He had lots of girls that worked for him and he only catered to the high dollar clients. She said his clients consisted of judges, senators, ministers and other very wealthy men.

Later in the afternoon Henry returned with Merci. He told Honey to get me dressed and ready. It would soon be time to deliver me to the judge.

Honey and I went in the bedroom. She brushed my long hair and then put it in pigtails. She held up one of the suits they had bought me. It looked like a uniform that a young girl would wear to school. After dressing, I looked in the mirror and I saw a young schoolgirl. I laughed to myself knowing I had never attended school my entire life. Very light makeup was applied. She said it was just enough to give me a nice glow.

She grasped my hand and led me to the other room. Henry looked at me as she turned me around.

He shook his head with approval and said, "Perfect, he'll love you. Okay, let's go."

Honey and I followed Henry as we went down the elevator and out to the street. The same shiny black car was waiting there for us. And the same man opened the door as the night before. It was already getting dark out. We didn't travel very far before stopping in front of another large building. The door was opened and Henry exited before me. Honey remained seated in the car.

She smiled and said, "You'll do fine. This is as far as I go. Good luck."

Henry held my hand like a person would hold their daughters hand as we walked through the lobby of the building.  It was really plush with lots of beautiful flowers, pictures and statues around it.  We entered the elevator and I saw Henry push the number fifteen on the panel.  When the door opened, we were not in a hall but stepped out into a big beautiful room.  The elevator came straight to his room only.  I thought to myself that the judge must be very wealthy indeed.

An older man was sitting on a big chair in the room.  He stood and motioned us to come in.  He smiled at me and said, "You're very pretty."

I replied, "Thank you, daddy."

He placed his hand on Henry's shoulder and said something I didn't understand.  I think he was expressing his approval of me.  He sat back down on the chair patting it to his side and motioned me to sit next to him.  Henry sat in a chair across from us.  The judge raised his hand and ran it down one of my long pigtails.  He reached inside a pocket of his jacket and pulled out a thick envelope, handing it to Henry.  Henry didn't open it but just put it in his jacket pocket.  He then stood and looked down at me.

In Chinese he said, "Don't screw up.  Make him love you and things will go good for you.  Do you understand?"

I nodded to him as if to say yes, but said nothing.

He started for the elevator saying something to the judge I didn't understand and then he entered the elevator and was gone.

I was very nervous as I sat next to the judge. I would have guessed him to be maybe in his sixties. He wasn't very tall and was pretty fat. He had a funny looking mustache and his gray hair was cut short and was very neat. He picked up a remote off the table and clicked it, causing a large TV mounted on the wall to come on. He had me to lay down on the chair with my head in his lap. He softly stroked my hair, while watching TV. He said nothing but continued stroking my hair as he watched the TV. I said and done nothing but just lay there.

Suddenly he bolted up from the chair dumping me to the floor. He grabbed me by the back of my shirt, all the time crying and yelling things I couldn't understand. He sat back in the chair pulling me by my pigtails, over his knees, face down. He grabbed my undergarments, ripping them off. He started spanking me hard and yelling at me at the same time. He stopped spanking and pulled me up to him. He was crying and he wrapped his arms around me.

As he hugged me he said, "I'm sorry. I'm sorry."

He said other things but I couldn't understand what was said. He then picked me up and carried me into another room. Lowering me on to a bed, he kept telling me how sorry he was. He removed all my clothes then covered me with a blanket. He leaned over and kissed my forehead.

He smiled down at me and said, "I love you."

I smiled back at him and said, "I love you, Daddy."

He turned and left the room, turning the light off as he did.

I lay there in shock.  I wasn't sure what had just happened.  I kept my eyes fixed on the door expecting him to come back at any time, but he never returned.  I thought about getting out of the bed and looking to see where he had gone or what he was doing, but I decided against it.  I lay there under the blanket, never taking my eyes off the open door.

At some point during the night I fell asleep.

When I awoke in the morning he was sitting on the bed next to me.  He softly stroked my hair and said, "Good morning."

I looked at him and forced a smile saying, "Good morning, Daddy."

He gently pulled me up to a sitting position on the bed.  He pulled the blanket from my body.  He never once looked at my nude body.  He grabbed a large thick robe from next to the bed and draped it around me.  He pulled me to my feet and hugged me.  While hugging me he led me back into the other room and onto a balcony.  A table on the balcony had plates containing fried eggs, toast, jam and big strawberries.  He pulled out a chair on the side of the table and sat me down.  He then sat in a chair across from me.

He motioned over the food and said, "Eat, eat."

I smiled and said, "Thank you, Daddy."

Not looking up at him, I began to eat the goodies in front of me.  Now and then I would glance over the wall of the balcony.  I could see across a large city.  In the not too far distance I could see a big river winding its way through the city.

His cell phone began to ring. Answering the phone, he looked at me with the sweetest smile. He handed me the phone. Placing it to my ear, I said nothing.

In Chinese I heard, "Good morning Rose. It's Henry. Good job. He likes you very much and wants you to stay the day and again tonight. Just keep doing what you're doing. He has to leave tomorrow morning and we'll pick you up. If you continue doing well you may never have to go back to Ms. Lee. Now give the phone back to the judge."

I handed it back to the judge and as he was talking to Henry I thought, *I have to go back, my money is in the air vent.*

After I finished eating, the judge led me, holding my hand, back through the bedroom to a large bathroom. He removed the robe from my body and turned on the water in the shower. After testing the water, he had me enter the shower. He never removed his clothes. Standing on the side of the shower he washed me with a large sponge and soap. He rinsed me off and grabbed a large fluffy towel and dried me off.

He dressed me again in a robe and hugged me asking, "You okay?"

I hugged him tight and replied, "Yes, thank you, daddy."

He led me back to the living room and turned on the TV. He sat me down on the big sofa across from it. He tuned it to an animated movie about a mouse. He crossed the room and sat at a desk. He started doing some sort of work and making calls on his phone.

I couldn't help but think to myself, *this is really weird. He was treating me like a daughter. No complaints from me, but really weird.* I sat watching TV for a long time. I didn't understand most of the movie, but that was okay.

He got up and went to a small kitchen on one side of the room. He poured a glass of coke and brought it to me. Handing me the glass he let it slip from his hand and drop to the floor. It didn't break but spilled its contents. It was so fast I didn't see it coming. He slapped me across the face and yelled at me. He grabbed me up and pulled me down across his knees as he sat on the sofa. He spanked me hard on my bottom, all the time yelling, "Bad girl, bad girl!"

He then pulled me up to him and hugged me tight saying, "I'm sorry. Are you okay?"

With tears flowing down my cheeks from the spanking I forced myself to say, "Yes Daddy. I'm Sorry."

He held me tight for a long time while rocking his body back and forth on the sofa. I could hear him crying the whole time.

I thought for a moment and said, "I love you, Daddy."

He hugged me tighter, with tears in his eyes, and said, "Thank you, thank you."

Again he picked me up and carried me to the bedroom. He lowered me on the bed and pulled the blanket over me. He kissed me on the forehead, turned and walked back to the living room. It was freaking me out. I lay in the bed for a long time with my eyes on the door. He never returned and I was too scared to go see what he was doing.

It was dark before he returned to the room. Turning on the light, he walked to the edge of the bed. He pulled the blanket off and pulled me up from the bed. He led me to the balcony again. The table was covered with plates of fried rice, a plate of boiled shrimp and plates of veggies. Again he pulled my chair out and helped me sit. I pulled the robe tight around my body while looking at the dishes on the table. I could see out across the city with lights everywhere. I could make out the river, covered with colored lights that seemed to follow the flow of the river. It was such a beautiful sight.

After the dinner he stood me in front of him, cupping my hands tenderly in his hands, he said, "Thank you, thank you."

He led me back to the bedroom. He removed the robe and laid me back on the bed. Covering my body with the blanket he kissed me on the forehead and again said, "Thank you Rose."

He turned and left the room, for the first time, closing the door behind him. I laid there for a long time before sleep came. That night I dreamed about living in the beautiful house. Mom was there with Bo and Su-Lin. Dad was there, he could walk and looked so healthy. We were all so happy.

## Chapter 9

"Wake up Rose, wake up.  Get up sleepy head."

I slowly opened my eyes to see Honey standing next to the bed.

She smiled and said, "Get up, get up, it's time to go."

As I climbed from the bed I thought, *it's good to hear Chinese again.*  She threw some clothes on the bed.  A pair of jeans, sweatshirt and a pair of loafers.  I threw the robe on the bed and got dressed.  She had walked back into the living room.  Walking back in the living room I seen Henry standing on the balcony talking on his phone.  The judge was gone.  Hanging up his phone, Henry walked into the living room.

Shaking his head and looking at me he said, "I don't know what you did.  The judge loved you.  He said you were the best of all the girls sent to him. What did you do?"

I just shrugged my shoulders and smiled.

He walked to my side and patted me on the top of my head, "Let's go."

They both, Henry and Honey, were in a happy mood as we left in the same car I had

arrived in the day before.

I kept hoping that Instead of taking me back to Ms. Lee, they would take me back to

the building where they lived. I found out when I had first arrived there that Henry didn't live

there. Only Merci and Honey, but I never seen Merci again. I didn't ask anything about her.

Honey showed me into the bedroom that had been occupied by Merci, telling me that she

wouldn't need it any more. She told me I would be living there with her. Henry would have

more clients for me and just keep doing what I was doing. She never asked me anything about

the judge or what we had done.

I stood, looking over the city, from my bedroom window. I couldn't see the river from

here but only lots of big buildings. I wondered if the other clients would be like the judge. I

hoped they would be.

I didn't have to wait long before my next customer. Henry delivered me to a large hotel,

not as nice as where the judge had been. I followed him to a room on the third floor. After

knocking, a man, maybe in his forties, that was well dressed with long hair to his shoulders,

fixed in a ponytail, opened the door. I noticed that he had a gold band ring on one finger on

his left hand. I knew that signified he was married. The room we were in was nice but nothing

like the room where the judge had stayed. There was no kitchen or living room. Just a large

room with a big bed, a small table with chairs and a bathroom on the side. He handed Henry an

envelope and then escorted him to the front door. Locking the door he looked at me and said,

"You're very pretty."

I was very nervous but said, "Thank you."

He walked to me and began undressing me. He pushed me back on the bed. I saw a round box high on the wall next to the bed. I stared at the box, trying to block out what was being done to me. When he finished, he climbed off of the bed and threw me my clothes as he walked into the bathroom with his cell phone. I could hear him talking to someone but couldn't understand what was being said. I dressed and sat in a chair next to the table. It wasn't long before there was a knock on the door. Coming out of the bathroom he pulled his pants on, throwing me a smile before opening the door. It was the man who drove the car for Henry. He motioned for me to follow him and we left the room. Sitting in the back of the car on the way home I hoped the judge would call again but he never did. I liked it better being with him than the other ones I was seeing.

I was seeing a different man every day. Some days I would have two clients. I began to realize that there was only one difference between Henry and Ms. Lee, with Henry, I was a higher prize piece of meat for men that didn't go to the massage parlors for different reasons. Many times I would sat at the house by myself because Honey would be out with a client. She didn't have clients every day but maybe three or four during a week. She told me once that Henry had no problem finding clients for me because of my age and they paid big money to be with me.

I had turned fourteen since coming with Henry. I was a little scared that I might not look as young as some clients wanted me too because I knew that when that happened he wouldn't need me anymore. The clients kept coming and I had been with so many men that I was numb, having learned how to block it out when I was with another one.

My fears kind of came true when Henry showed up at the apartment with a very young Chinese girl. Henry introduced her as Linn, who was eleven years old. He said she'd be staying with us and sharing the bedroom with me. She looked so small and innocent. I knew she would make a lot of money for Henry. I felt sorrow for her because I knew she'd never experience childhood. They had stolen that from her. I could see fear in her eyes as she sat in a chair while Henry talked to us. I showed her into the bedroom. She went to the window and while looking over the city, she cried. I walked to her side and put my arm around her trying to comfort her. I wanted to tell her that everything was going to be okay. I said nothing, knowing that it wouldn't be okay, but would get worse.

The next day Honey started coaching her for her first client. That afternoon she was dressed in a school uniform. She looked like an elementary school student. Honey said she was going to be with a wealthy doctor and he would be her first. I knew the doctor would reward Henry with a very large sum of money for Linn. Honey told me to get ready because I had a client too.

Henry picked us all up that night. Our first stop was at a very fancy hotel. There were water fountains in front of it and flower gardens along the front of it. The entrance had large gold pillars on both sides. A man in a gold uniform opened the car door when we stopped. As Henry and Linn exited the car Henry turned to me and told me to wait. Honey also stayed in the car with me. We exchanged no words but just sat in silence until Henry returned. Upon his

return we left and drove again.

Our next stop was another nice hotel. Honey sat in the car as Henry escorted me to a

room. After Henry knocked, a large man, maybe three hundred pounds or more, opened the

door. We entered the room as they talked. He gave a large envelope to Henry. Henry turned

and started out the door. I started backing away from the man to follow Henry as he went out

the door. The man grabbed me by the arm and pulled me back into the room as he slammed

the door closed behind Henry. His size frightened me and I kept trying to pull away from him.

He threw me on the bed and started removing his clothes. I jumped off of the bed towards the

door, but he hit me with an open hand knocking me to the floor. He laughed as he tore off my

clothes while picking me up and throwing me on the bed again. I attempted to scream as the

fear swelled in me. He cupped his hand over my mouth while kissing my body. I franticly

looked for something on the ceiling or wall to fix on. Seeing nothing, I closed my eyes as tight

as possible but couldn't block out the pain of what he was doing to me.

*Heavy fog all around me. People are talking but not to me. I hear loud noises.*

*Something being placed on my face. I hear someone yell something and then I feel something*

*hit me hard in the chest. It's starting to get dark and then it hits me in the chest again. Now the*

*fog again and lights in front of me. An image of a face in front of me, but something on my face*

*is blurring it more. Hard to breath. What's happening? Someone help me. Please help me. I*

*try to cry out for help, but nothing comes out. It's getting dark again and I try to yell for help,*

*but can't. Darkness and silence consumes me.*

84

As I awoke, I couldn't see anyone in the room. He was gone. I lay on the bed and cried. I feared he was in the bathroom and would be coming back. The door of the room opened and I grabbed the blanket and covered myself. I closed my eyes not wanting to see him again.

"He's gone," said Honey as she crossed the floor to the side of the bed. Handing me a change of clothes, "Here, put these on and let's go."

I glanced around the room to be sure he was gone before taking the clothes. I dressed quickly ignoring the pain through my body. I went to the bathroom and washed my face and arms. I could smell him on me. I wanted to take a shower but not there. I wanted to leave as fast as possible. I feared he might return. As we walked from the hotel to the waiting car I held my head down low. I didn't want anyone to see my swollen eyes, a result of crying and pain. Arriving back at our place we found it empty. Henry nor Linn had returned. I went straight to the shower. I soaped my body and stood under the shower for a long time.

Henry's driver came and picked up Honey later in the night. I sat on the sofa thinking about my life. I cried as I thought of mom, I missed her so much. I tried to think of a way I could go back to Hong Kong, but it seemed to be impossible. I kept trying to be strong, but it was hard to do. So many times I wished I would die because that may be my only way to escape. As I sat there, Honey and Linn came home. Linn didn't look at me as she crossed the room and went straight to the bedroom. I followed her into the bedroom as she was entering the shower. I stood by the shower and soaped her back for her and then washed her hair. She said nothing and just cried during the shower. I knew the pain she was feeling. I also knew that Ms. Lee had said I was no longer a child but was a woman. I thought she must be either blind or stupid because Linn and I were still children, being used and abused by some guy would not change that. After her shower she went straight to bed. I laid on the bed hugging her and stroking her hair until she fell asleep. It wasn't long before sleep came to me. My dreams that night weren't dreams but were nightmares. I relived the horror of the men I had been with and the abuse and pain I had suffered. I awoke during the night due to the screaming from Linn. Her dream had been a repeat of the abuse she had suffered that night. I held her tight as she fell asleep again.

When morning came we were both exhausted from the events and dreams from the previous night? Linn didn't want to leave the bed. I arose and walked into the living room. Honey was getting ready to leave.

I asked, "Where you going?"

In disgust she said, "I have an early client. Be back in a few hours. Watch over the kid until I return."

I nodded, "Sure."

After she left I looked in on Linn. She had fell back to sleep. Filling a bowel with steamed rice from the rice cooker on the counter, I sat next to the window looking over the city. I wondered what mom was doing. I wished this had all just been a bad dream and I would wake up in mom's arms back in Hong Kong. But in my heart I knew it wasn't a dream. It was a nightmare, but a nightmare I was really living. I wanted to escape but didn't know how and no one was coming to help me. I had a hard time understanding why Jesus didn't rescue me. If he really loved me then how could he let this happen? Su-Lin had told me before that Jesus loved us and would provide a better place for us. I didn't see how his love was doing a thing for me. I just couldn't understand it. I was strong when I started this experience and I was even stronger now, but Jesus had done nothing. I had suffered lots of pain and humiliation, but had grown stronger because of me, not Jesus. I knew that if I ever escaped from this horror I would have to do so on my own. I hated what I was being made to do, but feared what might happen to me if I was caught by the American police. I feared what might happen to Mom if I tried to escape and failed. My mind was full of horrible thoughts of things that could happen to me and Mom. I didn't know what to do.

"Rose, I'm hungry."

I turned to see Linn standing in the door of the bedroom. She looked so young and innocent. I thought to myself, *how could Jesus let her be used like this and be trapped in such a horrible life?*

Smiling at her I said, "Come, I'll fix you a bowel of rice with some veggies. Okay?"

She nodded to say yes.

She sat on the sofa, in silence, and ate the food. My heart hurt for her. I could see and feel that she was scared, confused and was with pain and shame. Even though I was only a few years older I felt much wiser and much older. I guess my life thus far had brought those feelings to me. She finished the bowl of food and just sat staring into the air. I took the bowl from her and sat next to her on the sofa.

Putting my arm around her I said, "It's going to be okay. I'll help you to be strong and survive. You can do it. You just have to learn to block out the pain and shame. You have to learn to be strong to survive."

She looked at me. Tears ran down her face and she said, "I hate her. I hate her."

"You hate who?"

"I hate my stepmother. She did this to me. Because of her, I'm here. I hate her. I hope she drops dead."

She opened up and proceeded to tell me about her life. Her mother had died giving birth to her. Her grandmother helped to raise her but when grandmother died it left the burden on her father. He tried his best to raise her while working a full time job. They lived in the coastal city of Wenzhou on the East China Sea. At the age of nine she was spending a lot of time at home by herself while her father was at work. He would rise early in the morning and prepare food for her and then get her ready for school. When she wasn't in school she stayed home by herself. Because of his worry for her, he remarried when she had just turned ten. Her step mother was cold toward her. She showed no love for Linn but sure loved the money her father brought home from work. Three months had passed since the accident. Her father worked on the docks at the shipyards. A container, being lowered from a ship, broke loose and fell on her father and two other men. They were killed instantly. Her stepmother showed no remorse over the death. She was more concerned that she had no money coming to her. One month after his death Linn turned eleven. One day a man from Shanghai visited her house. Her stepmother sold her to that man.  He took her to Shanghai where she was sold again and then put in a container, with a bunch of other girls, on a ship.

"Now, I'm here," she said as her voice trembled.  "I have nothing to go back too.  I have no family and no one cares what happens to me."

She put her face in her hands and started to cry.

Hugging her tighter I said, "You have me.  I care about you.  If you'll let me, I'll be your big sister.  Would that be okay?"

Looking at me with her eyes swollen from the tears, she said, "Yes, I'd like that."

We sat on the sofa for a long time holding each other.  Nothing else was said.  It was enough that we were there for each other to lean on.

I knew I couldn't stop them from using her for the sexual pleasure of their clients.  I knew I couldn't escape with her and run away.  But I knew that I could be there for her when she was brought back after each client.  I could show her love and try to ease the pain and shame that she would suffer.  I could give her a shoulder to cry on and know that someone cared.  I thought to myself, *Bo would be proud of me if he could see me. Standing up as a protector for someone, just as he had for me.*

A few hours passed before Honey came home.  Linn and I were sitting on the sofa watching cartoons when she came in.  She said nothing but went straight to her room.  I could hear the shower come on.  She came from the room dressed in a robe with her hair wrapped in a towel.  She seemed to be mad about something.  Maybe the client had been really bad.  I

89

didn't question her about the morning.  She fixed a cup of coffee and returned to her room,

closing the door behind her.

I looked at Linn, thinking maybe I should tell her about Jesus.  I said nothing because I

wasn't sure about him.  I didn't know if he was there for us or not.  I knew he hadn't helped me

yet.

Chapter 10



Almost every day one of us or all of us were picked up by Henry or the driver.  Some

days only one of us would have an appointment.  Linn was kept the busiest of us.  She was so

young that Henry probably worked hard setting up clients for her.  Being so young, she was

more in demand as a product.  She brought a lot more money than Honey or I.  I sometimes

wondered if having sex with young girls or kids was acceptable in American society.  It sure

seemed to be desired a lot.  I tried to always be there for her when she came home.  I would

help her shower and then to bed.  I would hold her in my arms until she fell asleep. Sometimes

she would tremble and cry out in her sleep from a bad dream.  I would just hold her tighter and

keep telling her she was okay.  She seemed to take comfort in the fact that I was there for her.

And honestly, it gave me a good feeling knowing that I was there.  I guess we both needed to

know someone cared and was there for us.

One night, after a few weeks had passed, Honey left for an appointment.  It was a rare

night because Linn and I had no appointments.  We watched TV and then went to bed.  The

next morning, Honey still hadn't returned.   Around eleven or so, Henry returned to the

apartment.  He was with a different girl.  He introduced her to us as Angel.  He told us that

Honey wouldn't be returning and Angel was in charge of the apartment.

When I asked him what had happened to Honey he said that she had moved to a different location. He talked to Angel, explaining what he expected of her. After he left, Angel told us to sit on the sofa. I could tell, she wanted to make sure we knew who was boss. She said that if we gave her any crap we'd regret it.

I asked, "What happened to Honey?"

She laughed and said, "She screwed up and pissed Henry off. She'll be pulling tricks in one of the brothels. There are lots of things he can do if you piss him off. He could even kill you if he desired. Honey might be better off if he'd have killed her. It would be better than where she was now."

"What did she do?"

With an evil grin she said, "None of your business."

With that said, she went into Honey's bedroom and closed the door. I would have guessed her to be about the same age as Honey, maybe twenty-two or twenty-three. She wasn't as pretty as Honey and she seemed to have a real bossy attitude. Linn and I glanced at each other, then continued watching TV. I thought to myself, *I will miss Honey. I liked her because she was always nice to us. I didn't think I was going to like Angel.*

Later that afternoon as it was growing dark outside, Angel emerged from the bedroom. She was talking on a cell phone and looking at us. She hung up the phone and said, "Henry called and said for Linn to get cleaned up and put on her school uniform."

Looking at me she said, "You too, put on your school uniform. He wants you both to put your hair in pigtails. He'll be here in a few to pick you up."

We were both sitting on the sofa, looking like a couple of school girls when Henry arrived at the apartment. He looked us over and then expressed his approval. We followed him out and down in the elevator to the waiting car in front. Once we were in the car he said, "This is something different for you. The client wants two schoolgirls at the same time. This guy is a big entertainer on TV. You may recognize him when you see him. He has lots of wealthy friends and is an important contact for me. Don't screw up. Treat him good and do what he wants. Got it?"

We both looked at him and shook our heads to say yes.

It was dark outside when we pulled up in front of the big hotel. Henry exited the car first, motioning us to follow. The hotel was very plush with beautiful pictures and statues in the lobby. In the elevator, Henry pushed the number fifteen on the control panel. Fifteen was the largest number on the panel so I knew from past experience it was one of the most expensive floors in the hotel. People paid a lot of money to be on the top floor and a room on that floor would be very spacious. Nothing was said as we went up in the elevator. Exiting the elevator we followed Henry to the very end of the hall. I noticed that there were only four doors in the hallway. I knew that meant there were only four rooms on the entire floor. After knocking on the door, to my surprise, it was opened by a young American girl. She smiled at us and motioned us to come in. Her hair was long and jet black. She had a number of tattoos on her arms and a tattoo of a Chinese symbol on her neck. We entered the room and were in a large living room area.  There was a bar on one side of the room with bottles of different liquors in stock.  Next to the bar was a door going to another room.  As we passed it I could see it was a bedroom.  On another wall was the largest TV I had ever seen.  Across the room on the other side was another door.  It was closed, so we couldn't see where it went.  She motioned for Linn and me to sit on a large leather sofa in front of the TV.  Henry followed her to the bar.  She poured him a drink from one of the bottles, as they talked.  Out the corner of my eye I seen her reach under the bar and retrieve a large, thick envelope.  It must have contained a lot of money.  Giving it to Henry, she laughed and said something I didn't understand.

Henry stuck the envelope in his pocket and then turned to us and said, "I'll see you later.  Remember.  Don't screw this up."

The girl walked him to the door and after he left she locked the door and went to a chair next to us and sat.  I was confused, I didn't know if we were there for her or who.  She said nothing but just sat there, sipping on her drink, staring at us.  As she stared at us I had a feeling that she was undressing us in her mind. It was a very weird situation.

The other door across the room opened and a young American man entered the room.  He wasn't very big but was very thin and muscular.  He wore only underpants exposing a large number of tattoos over his body.  He had tattoos on his arms, his back, his neck and a large tattoo of what looked like a cross on his chest.  He went straight to the bar and poured a drink from one of the bottles.  He walked to the chair on the other side of us.  He sat the drink on the table between us and then opened a large box sitting on the table.  He removed a small jar of what looked like sugar from the box.  Opening it, he then poured some on the table.  Using a knife he rearranged it in a straight line. He bent over the table with his nose to one end and

then moving along the line he sucked it up using his nose. I glanced at Linn sitting next to me on

the sofa. I could see her eyes were full of fear. He got up and walked straight to Linn. Taking

her by the hand he led her toward the room he had come from. I stood up to follow but the girl

stood up in front of me.

Putting her hand on my chest she pushed me back on the sofa. To my shock, she said in

Chinese, "You'll wait."

I was in shock. I had never heard an American speak Chinese.

After I sat back on the sofa she said, "You wait here. I'll come and get you shortly."

I was amazed at how good she spoke Chinese.

She followed them into the room, closing the door behind her. I sat on the sofa, trying

to hear what was going on as I looked around the room. My heart raced and my palms were

sweaty. I worried for Linn, hoping she was okay. Shortly, he came from the room. He was

nude and made no attempt to cover himself as he walked by me to the bar. He poured another

drink and went back into the room, closing the door behind him. I thought about moving to the

door to see if I could hear anything from the room, but decided against it. I sat on the sofa

staring at the door. I heard no screams or crying from Linn so I thought she must be okay.

The girl came from the room. She was also nude and as she passed me going to the bar

I could see a large tattoo covering most of her back. It was the tattoo of a man with wings

spread open and the head of a lion. She didn't have any fat on her. She was slim with a good

95

figure and her breast were large. She poured a drink and then went to the table by the sofa. She spread the white powder and then using the knife, she formed it into a straight line on the table. She bent over the table and made a snorting sound as she sucked it up into her nose.

Again in Chinese she said, "Wait, we'll be ready for you in a few."

I said nothing but watched as she went back to the room again closing the door behind her.

It wasn't long until she came from the room and taking me by the hand led me through the door. I backed up quickly but she wrapped her arms around me with a tight grip. Linn was laying on the bed. Her small body was nude, her hands and legs were tied to opposite poles on the sides of the bed. Her mouth was gagged. That explained why I had heard nothing from her. There were cameras in different parts of the room around the bed. The man pulled me from the girl and wrapped his arms around me. She stood in front of me and started kissing me on my mouth and my neck. He turned me around and she put police cuffs on my hands behind my back. She pushed me down on the bed and grabbed a knife from the table next to the bed. She started cutting my clothes from my body. She held me while he began to do things to Linn. I could see she had her eyes closed tight, trying to block out everything.

He took the knife and started cutting across her chest. Not deep cuts but just enough to cause slight bleeding. I tried to fight loose from the girls grip but she was too strong. I could see Linn screaming from the pain but nothing was heard due to the gag. I tried to kick him with my feet but the girl pulled me off of the bed and held me on the floor.

96

She grabbed my hair and pulled my head up to see Linn. In Chinese she said, "You'll watch or I'll cut her throat."

I opened my eyes and in horror watched as they did horrible things to Linn. I tried to yell for them to stop but they put a gag on my mouth. I continued fighting to get loose so I could stop them, but I couldn't. The man would cut her and then lick the cuts before licking Linn on the face. I had never seen anything so horrible in my life. They were monsters not humans. Surely no human could do this. The girl continued holding me and laughing the entire time. The bed was covered in blood. Linn opened her eyes and looked at me. In her eyes I could see she was begging for help but I couldn't do anything. Her tears mixed with the blood on her face. I felt so helpless and hurt inside. I wanted to help her, but couldn't. I didn't know what to do. All I could do was watch the nightmare take place.

The man got off the bed and stood over me as the girl held me. She pulled, holding me down as he lowered himself and started to rape me. I tried to block it out but could feel me screaming inside. After he finished, she moved in front of me. She held a large wooden item in her hand and pushed it into me. I screamed and she hit me with a closed fist. My last thoughts before blacking out was that someone had to help Linn.

When I woke up I was back at our apartment in my bed. I jumped from the bed and ran to the living room. Henry and Angel were standing by the sofa talking.

I yelled, "Where's Linn? Where's Linn?"

Henry looked at me and then turning his back to me said, "She won't be coming back."

97

Jumping on him, striking my fist with all my strength, at his back, "They killed her!  They killed her!  They killed her!"

He tried to throw me from his back but I felt the rage and hate strengthen me.  I clung on and kept hitting him in the back of the head.  I wanted to kill him.  Angel grabbed me by the hair and pulled me off of him.  He turned to face me, slamming his fist into my face.  I ignored the pain and kept fighting Angels grasp and swinging my fist at him.  I kept yelling at him, "I'll kill you!  I'll kill you!"

I saw his fist coming at me again.  The pain went shot from my head to my feet.

*The face was looking at me through the fog.  A light is hitting me in the eyes as the image in front of me is talking to me.  I can hear other noise around me.  I can't breathe!  I can't breathe!  Please help me!  I can't breathe!  What's wrong with me? Where am I?  Who are these people?  What are they doing to me?  Where am I?  Please help me!  I feel something being pushed down my throat and then a rush of air, I can breathe.  I hear, someone say in English, "You're okay."  I understood them.  They say I'm okay.  Who are they?  It's growing dark, dark and darker.  Now only darkness and silence surround me.*

# Chapter 11

I slowly opened my eyes but everything was so blurry. I could feel pain through my face from Henry hitting me. I hoped I had killed him, but I knew I hadn't. He sold Linn to them for their pleasure and they killed her. Why didn't they kill me too? He's no different than them. He's a monster. My heart ached with more pain than my face. They killed my little sister. They killed my friend. They killed Linn and I couldn't do anything to stop them. Why didn't they kill me? I would rather be dead than feeling this pain in my heart. I let her down. My eyes swelled with tears as I thought of Linn laying on that bed in a pool of her blood.

I wiped my eyes with my hands and tried to look around to see where I was. I could feel that my face was swollen from Henry hitting me. Between the swelling and the tears I couldn't see anything.

I heard a familiar Chinese voice, "Hey girl. You'll be okay. You're back with us now. Henry had a choice of killing you and throwing you in the dump or bringing you back here. I guess Ms. Lee told him if he ever tired of you, to bring you back. When he called her about what had happened, she told him to bring you back. For some reason she likes you."

I wrapped my arms around her and said, "Candy, is that you?"

"Yelp, in the flesh. Still hanging on here."

I cried as I said, "It was horrible. They killed her. They killed her. They killed Linn. Why's my life like this? Why do these things happen to me?"

"I don't know, but you're safe now. Ms. Lee said for me to take care of you until you're back on your feet. This isn't a free ride. You know you'll have to pay her back. It's strange, I have been with Ms. Lee for a long time and never seen her show heart for someone as she has for you."

She laid me down on my bedroll and began wiping my face with a cool cloth. As I laid there I could only think of one thing, *somehow, someday I would get him. I will somehow kill Henry for what he did to poor Linn.* Then the strangest thought entered my mind, *I hope she is with Su-Lin in heaven. Su-Lin will take care of her. But if Jesus and heaven is real why does he let these things happen. What kind of God lets little children suffer these kind of horrible things? What kind of God doesn't protect us if he loves us so much? Why doesn't Jesus help us? Where is he when we need him?*

I fell asleep as Candy held me in her arms. My dreams were bad. I could see Bo dying and then Su-Lin dying. But the worst was seeing Linn die and feeling so useless and unable to save her. My heart bled for her and it made me so sad.

When I woke up I realized I wasn't in the living area with the other girls. I was in the room that I had been locked up in when I first came to Ms. Lee. The difference was that the door wasn't locked. Candy would bring me food and hot tea during the day. When I had to go to the bathroom I went on my own to the one at the end of the hall not the one in the living area. I would return to the room and lay on the bedroll again. Every time I fell to sleep I would again go through the nightmares.  When I didn't sleep I had constant thoughts about things that had happened in my life.  I would think a lot about Mom and wonder how she was doing.  I wanted to go home to Mom and put this all behind me.   After a few days passed, Ms. Lee came into the room.

She sat on the floor across from me and said, "Are you ready to go back to work.  No clients for a few days, just laundry and cleaning.  If I hadn't had him bring you back here he would have either taken you to one of the brothels or just killed you and threw you in the dump.  You should be thankful you're back here."

I lowered my head and said, "Thank you, Ms. Lee.  I'll work hard and pay you back for your generosity.  I promise."

"Okay, rest more tonight.  Tomorrow, start back with laundry and cleaning."

She stood and went out the door, closing it behind her.  I didn't hear the lock turn in the door.  I knew that I wasn't locked in.  I laid down on the bedroll and hoped my money stash was still there.  That night I didn't dream about the people I had lost.  I dreamed about the yellow house with the beautiful flowers around it and the great front porch on it.

The next morning I woke up, picked up my bedroll and went to the living area at the front.  The parlor was still closed so everyone was there.  Ms. Lee was standing at the stove cooking eggs.  Candy was still sleeping.  There were three other girls sitting on their bedrolls watching TV.  I didn't see anyone I recognized.  The young girls that had first came with me were gone.  Candy was the only one that I knew.  I walked into the bathroom and stood in front of the mirror.  My face was bruised and still a little swollen.  As I looked into the mirror, hatred and rage began to burn in me again. I swore to myself that somehow I would get back at Henry for what he had done to Linn and me. Looking into the mirror I could see an image of Linn and the memory of what had been done to her was burned in my mind. For that I wanted to kill Henry. Some day he would get his.

Walking back in the living area, Ms. Lee pointed to the rice cooker and some eggs on a table and said, "Eat and then get to work. We were busy yesterday so there is lots of linen to wash."

I smiled at her and said, "Thank you, I will."

Before walking into the laundry room I looked behind to be sure no one was behind me. I went straight to the vent. Turning the knobs I pulled the grill off and reached deep inside. A feeling of joy shot through me as I wrapped my hand around the towel. I quickly removed it from the vent and found that the money was still rolled up in it. I had a good feeling when I placed it back in the hiding place and put the cover back over the vent. I walked to the dryer, removing the towels then moved the sheets from the washer to the dryer. Standing at the table I folded the towels.

Once we opened, the other girls were busy throughout the day. They were each taking care of six to seven customers through the day. I wondered what had happened to the girls that had first came with me but asked no one. Often during the day my thoughts returned to Su-Lin and Linn. I swore to myself that I would not get close to another person. It hurt too much to see them suffer or die. I had suffered enough and from now on I would just take care of me. I could not be a part of anyone else's suffering. My heart couldn't take it. There had already been too much pain in my life. I thought to myself, *I wish they had killed me along with Linn so there would be no more pain, no more suffering.* I couldn't understand why they killed Linn and let me live.

I tried to keep busy during the day cleaning and doing laundry to block out the image of Linn in my mind. It didn't work. The image wouldn't go away and it weighed heavy on my heart.

I spent the next couple of days cleaning and doing laundry. I said little to anyone around me. At night, after closing, I sat on my bedroll and watched TV with the other girls. They were friendly to me but no one asked me anything about what had happened. Candy would sit by me, on the floor, and try to comfort me sometimes. Ms. Lee would look at her and say, "Let her be. She'll be okay. Just leave her alone."

A few days passed and I started working customers again. I found it easy to block out their actions with me. I let them have their pleasure, but was only with them in body. My mind wandered to other places during those times. My body was the only thing on the table for their pleasure.

The other girls were glad I was there because it took some of the client load off of them. Some of the men I was with were customers I had been with before. Some would give me tips and I would add them to my stash in the hiding place.

A few weeks passed when two new girls were introduced to our parlor. I was in the laundry room when Ms. Lee met them at the back door. They were really young and as they came in the back door they were followed by the same two Chinese men that had first brought me to Ms. Lee. I peeked into the hall as Ms. Lee escorted them into the room where I had first stayed. I returned to doing some laundry.

Candy stuck her head in the laundry room and said, "Rose, you have a customer in room three. He wants our youngest girl and at the moment that is you. Be careful with him, he smells like a cop. I told him to undress and lay on the table."

Walking into the room, I was surprised to see him sitting on the table, fully clothed. He motioned for me to close the door. Closing the door I looked at him and said, "Hello."

He stunned me when he spoke in Chinese, "Hello, How are you?"

"A bit shocked to hear you speak Chinese. Where did you learn to speak ii?'"

"In a military language school in California. That was my job in the army."

I replied, "Wow! You speak it really good. What do you want to do?"

He smiled, "Just talk to you, if that's okay. What's your name?"

"Rose."

"No, I mean your Chinese name, please."

"My name is Mei-Lan."

"I like that. It means a beauty flower. I think an orchid. Right? My name is James. How old are you?"

I hesitated, "Fourteen. Are you a cop?"

He snickered, "No, not a cop." He softly touched my face, "But I do want to help you."

I walked to the table and turned on the CD player and set the timer to one hour. I walked back to the door and locked it. Turning to him I asked, "Do you want sex?"

"No, I'm not here for that. I want to talk to you and I would like for you to tell me about yourself and how you come to be here. Okay?"

My heart raced and I said, "I don't know. I'll get in trouble."

He motioned for me to sit on the table next to him and said, "No trouble, I promise, please."

Somehow I knew I could trust him and he was being honest with me. Maybe it was the way he spoke Chinese so well or just something I could see in his eyes. I asked him where he wanted me to start. He held my hand and told me to start at the beginning. I began telling him about my trip to America and all the horrible things that had happened. He reached over and grabbed some Kleenex off the table for me as I began to cry. He shook his head and I could see the sadness in his eyes as I told him about Su-Lin and what had happened to Linn.

The buzzer on the CD player went off and his hour was up. I didn't want to stop talking to him. It felt good inside to talk to someone about all that happened. He stood in front of me, holding my hands in his. He said he should go, so as not to create any suspicion. He explained that he wanted to help me and others but had to be very careful. The people that held me here were very organized and had ears everywhere. They even had police officers in their control.

He held my hands and said, "Mei-Lan, I promise.  I will help you.  I must go now but I'll be back."

I said, "Okay, I understand."

He grasped my hands and held them to his chest and in perfect Chinese, "Precious Jesus. You know Mei-Lan.  You know the pain she has and the suffering she has endured.  Lay your hands on her and give her comfort and peace in her heart.  Give her strength.  Show me the way to bring her and others out from this horrid life.  Bless her and shower her with your love..  In your precious name.  Amen."

There was a knock on the door and Ms. Lee asked, "Are you okay?  Your time should be up."

I dried my eyes and said, "Yes, he's just getting dressed."

She said, "If he wants more time, he needs to pay more."

He spoke up, in English, "No, no I'm finished."

He hugged me and kissed me on the top of my head whispering in my ear, "I'll be back."

As he opened the door I quickly turned and pulled the sheets from the table.  He walked out the door into Ms. Lee.  He thanked her and she smiled and escorted him to the front door.

I pulled clean sheets from under the table and recovered it.  I walked out of the room and glanced down the hall to see Ms. Lee showing him out the front door.   I walked straight to the laundry room, threw the sheets in the hamper, pulled clean sheets from the dryer and started folding.

106

As I stood folding the sheets, lots of thoughts went through my mind. Maybe I shouldn't have talked to him. Maybe I told him too much. What if he is just some weirdo and really didn't care what happens to me. What if he tells Ms. Lee? What if they come and get me to put me in a labor camp? I felt nervous that I had talked to him. But he prayed for me. Bad people wouldn't pray for me or would they?

I was so deep in thought that at first I didn't notice Ms. Lee come in the door. She was with two new girls. She introduced me to them. One's name was Cherry and she was only eleven. The other was called Baby, she was a little over weight, with a bit of a baby face. That's probably why they called her Baby. She was twelve years old. Ms. Lee told me to show them how the laundry was done. She said after that show them how to clean and what had to be done in a massage room, after a massage.

Ms. Lee walked to the shelf with the bottles on it and pulled it out. She opened the sliding door, while explaining when to go inside. She looked at me and said, "If we get raided you still need to go in. I don't want them to catch you and put you in a hard labor camp."

When she mentioned the hard labor camp I thought about the boy, James.

I spent the rest of the day showing the new girls what to do. I only had two customers that day, not counting James. I decided real quick that I didn't want to get close to the new girls. Everyone I became friends with, left me.

Two days later both of them had their first customers. My heart ached for them but I made sure not to let them know. When Ms. Lee brought Cherry back to the living area she was crying out loud. Hanging her head low with snot pouring from her noise and tears running

107

down her face    I felt I should go to her to put my arms around her and tell her that she would be okay.  I never moved, I just sat on my bedroll and tried to ignore her.  Candy came in to the room taking Cherry by the hand and leading her to the bathroom to help her take a shower. I was glad I was with a customer when Baby had her first.  Ms. Lee didn't give them to anymore customers that day.

The next day I was sitting on my bedroll.  Ms. Lee came in to get Baby for a customer.  Baby backed against the wall and yelled at Ms. Lee, "No, I won't do that again!  I won't do that again!"

Baby acted as if she was looking for somewhere to run away from Ms. Lee.  But before she got too far, Ms. Lee slapped her up side of the head.  Ms. Lee pushed her to the floor and started kicking her. "I spent a lot of money for you and did you a favor by bringing you in my parlor.  You will work or I can sell you to someplace else.  If you go there you will work and not even know you are working.  You can do twenty men a day.  I promise, you won't remember any of them." Ms. Lee grabbed her by the hair and dragged her, kicking and screaming, down the hall and into the other room.

Ms. Lee came back to the living area and went to the closet.  I knew she was going for the big stick.  Her cell phone went off.  She listened to someone on the other end and then put the phone in her pocket.  Looking around the room she yelled, "Rose, Cherry go to the secret room.  Now! Hurry! Candy, come help me!"

Cherry and I ran to the secret room behind the shelves.  Ms. Lee and Candy dragged Baby to the room.  I sat on the floor in the room as Candy held Baby while Ms. Lee pulled a syringe from her pocket and jabbed it into Baby's arm. I don't know what it was, Baby slipped into unconsciousness real fast. They dragged her into the room with us and then Ms. Lee said, "Don't move, don't make any notice, don't come out until we come for you. We can't let them find you. These are really bad cops and they will hurt you bad for being in America illegally. I will protect you."

She pulled the sliding door shut and then I heard the shelf being pushed against the wall. It was dark in the room. I couldn't see the other girls. Nothing was said and the only sound in the room was Baby breathing heavy. It wasn't long before I could hear commotion in the room. People were talking but I couldn't understand everything they were saying. I could hear Ms. Lee yelling at them. I think she was complaining about them coming into her business.

We were in the room for a long time before I heard the shelf being moved from the door. The door slid open and Ms. Lee was standing in front of us. Candy and Ms. Lee dragged Baby from the secret room down the hall to the other area. I stood in the hall and Ms. Lee came out locking Baby in the room. I heard her tell Candy that she would deal with her later.

She walked straight to me. Before I seen it coming she slapped me on the face, knocking me back against the wall in the hall.

With an angry voice, "What did you tell him?"

Holding my face I said, "Who?"

"The man, the man you had a couple of days ago. He was with them. They were specifically looking for underage illegal aliens"

I said, "I said nothing. He spoke Chinese so we talked more than most of my customers but I told him nothing." I hoped she wouldn't sense I was lying.

"Did he do you?"

"What?"

"Did he have sex with you?"

I lowered my head to hide my eyes from her, "Yes. Yes, we had sex."

She slapped me again saying, "I better not find out that you're lying to me!"

I leaned against the wall, my legs trembling, my heart racing. She turned and walked back to the living area. As she passed the room with Baby locked inside she paused. Spouting obscenities in Chinese and English, she proceeded to the front area.

Instead of going to the living area I turned and went back to the laundry room. I pulled towels from the dryer and started folding. I didn't know what James had told the police. I don't think he told them my name or any of the information we had talked about. If they had asked where I was by name, Ms. Lee would have known I lied to her. She would beat me to a slow death. Like all of the other girls, I stayed away from Ms. Lee for the rest of the day. We knew she was pissed and didn't want to be on the receiving end of the stick. When I wasn't with a customer, I stayed in the laundry room.

I couldn't get James out of mind. He seemed so sincere. I thought he would help me. I thought he could free me from this lifestyle. I thought for a while that escape from this was possible. I, down deep, had hoped that at last I would be free. Maybe I should have come out of the secret room while they were here.  Maybe he would have taken me with them.  But I didn't know he was with them.  Maybe if he had called my name, I would have known.  I think he didn't call my name because he was afraid to alert them.  Ms. Lee would have known that I had talked to him about everything.  Yes, that's why he didn't dare call my name.  I wondered if he was a cop or what.

That night after closing Ms. Lee was still very mad.  She met two Chinese guys at the back door and they took Baby with them.

The next few days went as normal.  I was working six to seven men each day.  The majority of them were there for sex but a few just wanted a good massage.  I even had some that never took their underpants off.  I was happy when all they wanted was a massage.

About three days after the police raid I seen John, Ms. Lee's police friend, come in the front door.  They stood talking for a while and then she went and brought Cherry out to meet him.  He held her hand and took her to one of the rooms.  I thought to myself, *probably his pay for information.*

After they went into the room I went to the laundry room to check the dryer.  Ms. Lee followed me in.

I heard her say, "He wasn't a local cop.  He is some kind of federal cop.  He works with a unit that looks for young girls that are working as prostitutes." She laughed, "You're not a whore.  You're a masseuse.  You know we never have sex with our customers.  Right?  Only massage.  If they don't ask for it or do something to indicate they want sex, they only get massage.  Right?"

"Yes ma'am."

"We have to be more careful. I must talk to all the girls. They will be watching us more. Good thing I have friends on the police force."

She grunted, turned and walked from the laundry room.

That night, after closing. Ms. Lee gathered us all together. First she repeated what she had told me earlier about being careful. She also told us to never give our Chinese name to a customer or tell them anything about our life.

Her face got a serious look, "You don't want to be here. You don't want to do what you do. I tell you this because someone may come as a customer and tell you lies to get you to talk to them. Don't trust them. The only way they will help you is lockup in a hard labor prison for the rest of your life. I am the only one you can trust. True, I own you. But there are a lot worst places you could be working." She grunted and shook her head, "Baby will know that now. After she does fifteen to twenty men a day she will be wishing she was back here. I will protect you from the authorities and the prison camps. I will take care of you. In return you work hard, do what I tell you to do, make the customers feel good so they come back and never tell me no or give me any crap."

She turned from us and walked back into the hallway.

With a sigh of relief I thought, *James said nothing about me. He told my name to no one. If he had, John would know and he would have told Ms. Lee. I wouldn't be here now. I would have left with Baby. Maybe he would find some way to help me yet. I hoped so.*

Chapter 12

Not even a week after Baby had left, two more new girls arrived.  They were not as young as most.  They were probably sixteen to seventeen.  That made six girls, the youngest being Cherry, working for Ms. Lee.   I was actually glad because most days, with two more girls, I only had to service three or four men.

Ms. Lee gave them the same speech, she would protect them from prison, she would take care of them, don't piss her off or else.  Just do your job and everything would be good.

When I received tips I would put it in my stash behind the grill in the vent. I was amazed, I was up to eight-hundred dollars.  I was very careful to always be sure no one was around or coming down the hall.  I wasn't sure what Ms. Lee would do if she found it.  The other girls must get tips too.  Surely Ms. Lee knew that we received tips.  Maybe she didn't care.

One night as I lay on my bedroll, I heard a familiar voice.  Anger boiled up in me and my heart began to race out of control.  It was Henry.  I could barely hear him and Ms. Lee talking about Cherry.  I didn't move but remained still.  I wanted to jump on him and try to kill him.  I wanted to scratch out his eyes.  I wanted to rip his heart from his body.  It was hard, but I forced myself to remain still as if I was sleeping.  Somehow I knew that someday he would receive his.

Ms. Lee walked Cherry over to him.  After introducing her to him they talked for a little and then left together.  I wanted to scream out to her, *don't go with him,* I didn't.

Sleep eluded me that night.  Memories of Linn flooded my mind.  Tears burned my eyes and rolled down my face as I thought of her.  Every time I closed my eyes, I could see Linn tied on the bed and they were cutting her little body.  Henry sold her to them.  He knew what they wanted to do.  He knew what their pleasure was.  He didn't care.  If the money was right is all he cared about. He sold her life to those people.  I wanted to see him die so much.  I found myself praying that someone would kill him.  The only thing that would please me more would be able to watch or do it myself.

A day didn't pass that I didn't think of Mom, I missed her so much.  I hoped she was doing okay.  I wondered what she thought, not having heard from me for almost two years.  Two years, it's hard to believe I've been in America for almost two years.

Sometimes I thought about James.  Was he looking for me or did he give up on finding me. Should I have come from the room during the raid, I don't know.  I'll never know.  If the opportunity presented itself again, I would take my chance with the police.

The two new girls came from another parlor.  They didn't say much.  They kept to themselves.  I didn't question them about their life.  I didn't want to get involved with anyone else.  It hurt too much when you lose them.

114

Weeks passed, never seeing Cherry again. *Maybe she met the judge. I wish all my customers were like him, or even better like the old man that fell asleep on the table.*

One day, after a customer, I was taking the sheets to the laundry room when I heard a blood curling scream come from the living area. Ms. Lee came running from the laundry room yelling, "What now?"

I threw the sheets in the laundry room and ran behind Ms. Lee. Candy and Suzy, one of the new girls, were standing in the doorway of the bathroom. Their faces were as white as the sheets we used on the tables. Suzy was trembling as Ms. Lee pushed her aside and went into the bathroom.

As I walked up to stand behind Candy I heard Ms. Lee, "Oh my god."

I peered around Candy to see the other new girl, Jackie, laying on the floor of the shower. The water was turning red as it mixed with her blood going down the drain. Ms. Lee turned off the water and picked up a razor blade from the shower floor. She turned and yelled at us, "Get out! Close the door!"

Backing out of the bathroom I could see Jackie staring at us. She had a blank expression on her face.

With the door closed, Candy turned and said, "She took the coward's way out."

"What do you mean?" I asked.

"She didn't want to live in this life any longer, so she killed herself." Candy replied.

Confused I said, "But she's not dead. I saw her moving."

115

Candy grunted and started walking to the hallway, "She's as good as dead. She'll never come out of that shower alive. She'll bleed out."

I asked, "They'll take her to the hospital. Right?"

Before walking into the hall she turned with a sad look on her face and grunted, "Not hardly. The only place she'll go is to the dump."

I have seen death but not death when someone took their own life. Jackie wasn't dead when I saw her on the floor. I knew she would die. Ms. Lee would let her bleed out. There was no help for her. I didn't really understand, why would someone take their own life? Candy had said, it was the coward's way out. But I thought, *Maybe Jackie wanted out so bad, that's the only way she thought she could escape.* Not me, I wasn't a coward and I could never take my life. I would rather someone kill me.

Ms. Lee told us to not go into the bathroom until told different. We were to use the restroom at the other end of the hall by the laundry room. I was in the laundry room when Ms. Lee opened the back door. Two Chinese guys came in and followed her to the front. When they passed by on their way out they were carrying a large black bag. I knew, Jackie's body was in that bag. I thought to myself, *she escaped.* After locking the back door, she stuck her head in the laundry and said, "Rose, go clean that bathroom. Use towels and liquid cleaner. After you finish, throw those towels away. Got It?"

I replied, "Yes ma'am."

There was blood all over the shower and bathroom floor. As I began washing down the floor of the shower, my thoughts went back to the day Bo died. I thought of Bo's blood mixing with the rain on that street. It had been over two years, almost three years, since that day. It still weighed heavy on my heart, but not like before. I had been exposed to and seen so many bad things since then. I didn't know if I was becoming stronger and tougher or just dying inside.

After cleaning the floor, I leaned back against the wall. Thinking about all that happened to me, I sat there staring at the shower.

*"Mei-Lan,"* a soft voice said. *"Don't give up. Have faith. You will escape if you remain strong. We are always with you. You're not dead inside. You're strong and will become stronger. Don't lock Jesus from your life. You may feel he has deserted you. He hasn't left you. He will always be with you. He loves you and will always walk with you."*

My body jerked as I suddenly opened my eyes. I looked around the small bathroom. No one was there. I had fell asleep and dreamed it. Or had someone been there for real, talking to me? I felt a warm feeling pass through my body. My thoughts went to Su-Lin, she loved Jesus so much. She had so much faith in him and his word. I wanted to be like her, but it was hard. He had not talked to me. I had never seen him. I wanted to believe he existed, but so hard. I couldn't understand how he let me suffer so much and be used so much if he really loved me.

It was a slow day. Not too many customers came that day. I was happy about that.

With Jackie and Cherry gone it left only four of us to take care of customers. There were no questions or talk about Jackie after that day. I'm sure everyone wondered about where they took her, as I did, but no one asked. Candy had said they would take her to the dump. I wondered what that was and where it was.

Working in the laundry room one day with Candy, I asked, "Candy, what is the dump they take people to?'

"It's a dump. A trash dump. It's just outside of the city. It's where they take all the trash from the city. If one of the girls dies she goes to the dump. They put her in a big bag and throw her body in with all the trash there. The people working, push dirt over the trash every day. No one will ever know there's a body mixed with the trash. Even if they did find her body, it wouldn't matter. There's no ID, no record for that girl. No one knows we are here but the people we work for. If they find a body they will probably give it a proper burial. And that's good, I guess. They'll never know who she was."

Shaking my head I said, "That's terrible. Her family will never know what happened to her."

Candy mumbled, "No one will ever know, my family, your family, where we are or what happens to us. They'll never know."

I said, "I don't want to just be thrown in the trash."

She snickered, "Then you have to be like me. I don't like what I do. I want to escape from this life too. I won't kill myself to do that, I don't think that's right. I just don't rock the boat or make trouble. Maybe someday I will have the opportunity to escape, I hope. You can bet that if I ever have the chance, I'll jump on it"

118

I said nothing else. I went back to folding sheets and thinking about what she had said. I thought of that as a good day. I only had two customers. Of course, Ms. Lee likes it when we are very busy, that's more money for her.

Not too many days passed before new girls arrived. Two new ones arrived, both in their early twenties. I think they had come from another parlor. Their names were Lisa and Amber.

They fit in fast. They knew how to greet the customers. Especially Amber, she was always so friendly and happy. Either she liked what she was doing or put on a great show for us. For sure, they had been working someplace before.

Business began to pick up again. Even with six girls we were doing seven or eight a day, Ms. Lee was very pleased. I knew from the time I worked for Henry, we were in a big city. Clients were plentiful. One thing I noticed was repeat customers. A lot of the men visited us repeatedly and often.

I would be turning fifteen soon. Almost three years since I arrived in America. Three years of hell. Three years of shame and pain. Maybe Jackie took the right option. At least she had escaped. No more pain or suffering for her. I began to think about ways of taking my life and ending the suffering. Bleed out in the shower, no to messy and to slow. Take too many drugs, no, didn't have access to any. Piss off Ms. Lee really bad so she'd kill me. I knew down deep in my heart I couldn't do it. I couldn't take my life. Candy had said it was the coward's way out. And I wasn't a coward. I would find another way.

## Chapter 13

My fourth customer of the day had just left. I pulled the sheets from the table and clutching the twenty dollar tip in my hand, went to the laundry room.

I glanced back to be sure no one was behind me. Pulling the grill off the vent, I pulled out the towel with my money wrapped inside it. I began to count it.

"What's that?" Amber was standing in the doorway of the laundry room. Again, "What is that?"

I clutched the money tightly in my hand and held it behind my back, from her sight, "Nothing, just a dirty towel."

She smiled and said, "Yeah, right. I saw the money. Where'd you get that money? Did you steal from Ms. Lee?"

"No, I didn't steal it! They gave it to me. Customers gave it to me."

She came across the room faster than I thought possible. Grabbing the money from my hand, she said, "It's mine now and I won't tell Ms. Lee what you were doing."

I yelled, "No, it's mine."

120

I jumped at her trying to grab the money.  She was bigger than me and pushed me back.  I hit the table in the middle of the room, knocking it across the room.  I jumped up and started at her again.

"Hey, what's going on?" Yelled Ms. Lee, standing in the door of the laundry room.

Amber and I both looked at her in shock.  Amber, handing the money to Ms. Lee said, "Ms. Lee, I found her hiding this money from you.  I was getting ready to bring it to you when she jumped me, trying to stop me."

I didn't know what to say.  My heart was racing so fast I could hardly breathe.

Ms. Lee asked, "Rose, where did you get this money?"

I started to cry and said, "My customers gave it to me.  It's my money.  I didn't steal it. I promise."  I thought fast and said, "I was going to save it up and give it to you to pay off my debt to you.  I was going to pay you, so I could go home.  Please, Ms. Lee, let me go home." With tears streaming down my cheeks I begged, "Please let me go back to my Mom."

She looked at me with a serious look, "Rose, You have nothing to go back to.  I'm sorry, but your Mom died over a year ago."

I felt my legs go weak and I sank to the floor, "No, no, please let me go home.  She's not dead.  She's there and will be glad to see me.  I know she's not dead."  Sitting on the floor with my head in my hands, I cried out, "No, she can't be dead!  You're lying!  She's not dead!  You're lying!"

121

She said with a soft voice, "I'm sorry.  I have no reason to lie to you.  I'm sorry."

She turned and walked from the room.  Amber snorted and followed her out.  I rolled into a ball and cried harder as I lay on the floor.  Ms. Lee came back in the room, accompanied by Lisa and Candy.  Candy sat on the floor and pulled me to her, hugging me tight.  Ms. Lee grabbed my arm as Candy held me.  I felt the needle enter my arm.  I slipped into unconsciousness.

*It was my eleventh birthday.  Mom and Bo were laughing as we ate the cake Mom had brought home.  Mom gave me the beautiful yellow head scarf.  She tied it around my head and told me how beautiful I was.  She said I was her beautiful orchid flower.  Bo laughed as I unwrapped the present from him.  It was the picture of the beautiful house he had glued to a white cardboard.  He said it was the house I would live in someday.  He hugged me and told me how he loved his little sister so much.  It was a great time.  Sitting with Mom and Bo on my eleventh birthday.  Things started to become foggy.  A thick, heavy fog settled around me.  I can't see Mom or Bo.  There are lights in the fog.  An image of a face is in front of me.  I can't make out who it is.  I know it's not Bo or Mom.  I can hear them talking, but I can't understand them.  The lights are getting dark.  It's growing dark, dark and only darkness now.*

It was hard to open my eyes.  They seemed so heavy.  I heard someone talking.  It was Candy and Ms. Lee. I opened my eyes to see I was on my bedroll in the living area.  The TV was on and only Candy and Ms. Lee were in the room.  Candy was sitting next to me on my mat.  She stroked my hair and said, "You're okay.  You'll be fine."

I pulled myself up to sit on the bedroll. Candy handed me a hot cup of tea and said' "Drink this. It'll make you feel better."

I took the cup and held it with both hands. Sipping at it did feel good. It felt good going down my throat. I looked around the room to see Ms. Lee, she was gone. I asked, "What happened?"

She smiled and said, "She gave you a shot to knock you out."

"How long have I been out?"

"Two days. You talked in your sleep. You were talking to your Mom and someone named Bo."

"That was my brother. He died in a street fight, back in Hong Kong."

I sensed genuine sincerity as she said, "I'm sorry. I'm really sorry about your Mom too."

With tears slipping down my cheeks I said, "Why? Why was I never told?"

She explained, "They don't care. They don't care about you, your family or your feelings. The only thing they care about is that you are able to provide a service to their customers and the money they make from that. Honestly, you're lucky to be here with Ms. Lee. She still just thinks of you as property, but differently. Like a good TV or anything else she will take care of you in order to get the most she can from you. Other places don't even take care of the girls. They keep them drugged up and working. At fifteen to twenty men a day, a girl doesn't last long. Most of the time they don't even know when a man is with them."

I asked, "How long have you been doing this?"

She shook her head, "I came here when I was fifteen. I'm twenty-one now, so about six years. I have always been with Ms. Lee. She's kind of like family to me. I grew up in an orphanage in China. After being adopted at age fifteen, they sold me to a man a few months later, he sent me here. I don't know anything else. I don't enjoy what I do but it's what I do. The best thing that could happen to me is to maybe someday be a mamasan in an establishment. Ms. Lee started the same way you and I started. Look at her now. She makes money and doesn't have to pleasure the men any longer."

"What about my money? Will she keep it or give it back to me?"

"I don't know," shaking her head, "She'll probably keep it, but sometime, when she is sure she can trust you, she will take you with her to go shopping. We've went to a nice place to eat and went shopping together. She bought me new clothes. I think she likes you or she would've never let you come back after the incident with Henry. I keep telling you girl. Don't rock the boat. Just do your job and you'll be okay."

The door opened and Amber walked in. She looked at me but said nothing. I threw a cold stare at her as she crossed the room and went into the bathroom. She lowered her head, not wanting to look at me.

Candy patted me on the leg and said," Forget it. She's not worth getting into trouble over. She'll get it someday." She got up and started walking from the room. She winked at me and said, "Remember, don't rock the boat."

124

I didn't have any customers that day. I guess Ms. Lee gave me the day off. I spent most of the day sleeping. Maybe the shot she gave me hadn't wore off yet. My dreams that day were about Mom, Dad and Bo. We may have not had much but we did have a lot of love and we had each other.

To my surprise, the next morning I woke up feeling refreshed and very strong. Even more to my surprise, Ms. Lee walked in and told me to come and go with her. Not knowing what to expect I followed her out of the living area. I looked at Candy, standing at the stove, and she winked at me.

We went out the door and a taxi was waiting for us. Ms. Lee motioned for me to enter the taxi and then followed me in. She said something to the driver and we were off.

I asked, "What are we doing?"

She smiled at me and said, "Shopping, we're going shopping."

I sat back in the seat. Looking out the window, I saw lots of cars and people walking. Lots of stores and big buildings. I knew it was a big city but never realized it was this big. We drove for a long time before we entered a parking lot in front of a huge facility. The taxi pulled up in front of a big entrance area and stopped. I asked Ms. Lee what it was and she said it was a shopping mall. I was in awe as we walked through the entry. I had never seen anything so beautiful. Flowers and plants were everywhere. We walked along a long corridor with different types of stores on both sides. There were smaller places set up in the corridor, selling sunglasses, cell phones and all sorts of things. It was an amazing place.

We walked up to an entry door and Ms. Lee opened the door and motioned me to enter. Immediately, a wonderful smell filled my nose. It was a restaurant, it smelled great, even better, it was an Asian restaurant. We were met by a young lady, dressed in a gorgeous Chinese dress, who directed us to a table. I have never ate that good in my entire life.

As we ate, Ms. Lee said, "Rose, I want you to know, I am truly sorrow about your mother. I'm sorry not to have told you before, but it wouldn't have made any difference in your situation. I like you. You remind me of me. I came to America twenty-three years ago. My family paid a man to bring me into this country so I could get a better education and make a good life for me and my family. They paid a down payment to the man but were unable to pay off the balance. Because of that, I was forced to work in massage parlors. I was lucky, I had some good mamasan's. They took care of their girls, just as I take care of mine. There were not as many girls brought over in those days as today. There were no cheap, dirty brothels that I knew of, where girls were forced to work. There were only the massage parlors. Today is different. There is a steady flow of girls from all over Asia. They work in massage parlors, escort services and the really unfortunate ones are in the cheap brothel houses. It is big business and some people make lots of money in it."

I questioned, "What about you? You make lots of money. Lots of men come to the parlor."

She grunted and said, "I wish. Most of money goes to the people that own the parlor. I'm a prisoner there, just as you. Sure, I don't have to pleasure the customers. At the age of forty-five, I have nothing else I can do.  I could leave if I wanted, I think, but to do what?  I consider myself lucky.  I could be buried in a dump someplace, like so many other girls."

She reached across the table and squeezed my hand, "Believe me. I know how you feel. I've been there.  If there was any way I could give you, Candy, and the others a better life, I would do it.  But sadly, it's not mine to give."

I placed my hand on hers and said, "I understand. I really do.  Thank you."

Nothing else was said and we finished our meal.  Leaving the restaurant, I followed her to a women's clothing store.  She bought me a couple of pairs of jeans, a few shirts, some shoes and one very short, very sexy looking dress.

We walked through the mall for a while.  I was amazed at what I saw, beautiful clothes, and shoe stores, stores full of all sorts of electronic stuff, bookstores, and different types of food places.  Eventually, we went out and got another taxi.  On the way back to the parlor we went a different route.  We were driving along the river I had seen from Henry's place.  It was so beautiful.  Arriving back at the massage parlor, Ms. Lee paid the taxi and I followed her back inside.

Candy opened the door from the lobby area into the parlor.  She patted me on the back and asked, "You okay?"

I smiled at her and said, "Yes, I'm good."

I watched Ms. Lee as she walked the hall toward the bathroom at the back. I looked at Candy as she returned to the living area. I was sure the other girls were all with customers. I thought to myself, *is this it. Is this all I have left in life. Is this all the family I will ever have now?*

With that thought in mind I felt sick. I knew I could never accept this life as Candy and Ms. Lee had accepted it.

A few days later, while working with Candy in the laundry room, I asked, "Candy, have you heard about Jesus?"

The question must have caught her by surprise, "Yeah, I guess. When I was in the orphanage they told us about God and Jesus. Why do you ask?"

"Do you think he's real? Do you believe in him and his word? I'm just curious, what do you think about him?"

She paused and then looked straight at me, "Yeah, I believe he's real. I don't remember much of his word. I remember being told about how he died on a cross and then I think, three days later, arose from the grave. They said he went to heaven to be with the father. I remember, someone told me that he died for us."

"Do you think he really loves us, as they say?"

She lowered her head, "No, how could he love us? I don't think he'd want anything to do with someone like me. I know enough to know that I have lived in sin for a long time."

I interrupted, "But we don't live in sin by our choice. Doesn't that make a difference?"

"I don't know, but I don't want to talk about it. Okay?" She said as she turned and left the room.

I liked Candy. She had become like a big sister to me. I decided then, I wouldn't say anything else to her about Jesus. I didn't want to make her mad or upset with me. She was the nearest thing I had to family. I wasn't sure myself, not knowing how I felt about Jesus. Maybe he didn't love us because of what we were doing.

Weeks passed, we had busy days and other days that very few customers came. Some days, I had no customers and I liked that. I was glad I was with Ms. Lee for the time being. I knew there were a lot worst places to be. Nothing changed much for me. I was still giving pleasure to five or six men on a normal day. It didn't bother me much because I had learned to block out everything that happened. If I received any tips from customers I gave it to Ms. Lee. I was surprised, sometimes she told me to keep it for our next shopping trip.

## Chapter 14

It was late night, almost closing time.  It had been a busy day.  I had been with five men during the day and was really tired.  Everyone had been busy all day.  I turned fifteen today and I thought of how it had been four years since my last birthday party.  The party with Mom and Bo on my eleventh birthday.  I saw Ms. Lee escort our last customer out the front door and then she turned off the lobby lights, after locking the door. I was taking the last load of dirty sheets from a room to the laundry room.

Candy stuck her head in the laundry room and said, "What did you do now?  Ms. Lee says for you to bring your butt to the front, right now, hurry." Without another word, she took off up the hall to the front.

I followed, almost running, to the living area.  I kept thinking, *what's wrong?  What did I do?  Was I in trouble?*

I rushed through the open door and then took a few steps back from what I saw.  They were all standing together in the middle of the room and started singing happy birthday to me.

Ms. Lee was holding a cake with candles on it blazing away. I stood frozen in place, not believing what I was seeing. I started to cry from the joy that filled my heart.

Candy put her arm around me and laughed, "Why are you crying?"

With tears in my eyes and a smile on my face I said, "I guess I'm happy."

We ate cake and laughed about my reaction, coming in the room. There were no presents but that was okay. Even Amber smiled and told me happy birthday. It was a good night because I was happy and felt loved. I also felt like I had a family again. Yes, it was a good night.

It was strange when Amber disappeared. She had been with a repeat customer. He always asked for her when he came in. Her hour with the customer had passed. Ms. Lee went knocking on the massage room door. I heard Ms. Lee calling for Amber. Ms. Lee had already checked the laundry room and the bathroom at the back of the parlor. She came into the living area and went straight to the restroom.

She came out with a bewildered look and asked, "Have you seen Amber?"

I shrugged my shoulders and said, "No."

"Where did she go?"

I replied, "Don't know, Ms. Lee. I haven't seen her."

I followed her as she went to every empty massage room, looking for Amber. She even knocked on the doors that were occupied asking, "Amber, are you in there?"

The answer was always no. Candy came out of a room and escorted her customer to the front. After he left, she asked, "What's going on?"

Ms. Lee said, "Amber is gone. She must have left with the customer. She's so stupid."

Ms. Lee pulled her cell phone from her pocket and started punching numbers. She walked back down the hall to the living area.

I asked Candy, "Who is she calling?"

"Probably John or one of the other cops that she's in good with. They'll put out some sort of alert about her, maybe a missing persons or something. She must have went with her customer. Ms. Lee will also, more than likely, call Henry."

Confused, I asked, "Why Henry?"

"You haven't figured it out by now. Ms. Lee answers to Henry. He's her boss."

"So he owns this parlor?" I asked.

"No, but he works for the people that do. They'll want to find her before anyone else does. She knows too much about what goes on here. If the wrong authorities were to get hold of her, they'd shut this place down and make big problems for Henry."

Ms. Lee came from the living area, "Candy, go lock the front door, turn off the open sign and turn the lights off in the lobby area. Henry says for us to close until further notice. Go, hurry, hurry!"

She looked at me and the other girls and said, "Go clean all the rooms and then come to the living area."

Without questioning her, we did as she said. It was only 9:00, three hours before we normally closed. After all the rooms were cleaned we went to the living area.

In the living area, we started fixing something to eat. Ms. Lee sat on the floor, holding her cell phone, waiting for a call.

A few hours had passed, her cell phone rang. She listened for a moment and then jumped up and went to the back door. When she came back in the room she was with John, her cop friend. He had a little notebook in his hand and was writing. He looked at us and started talking. Ms. Lee stood next to him and translated to Chinese, so we would understand what he was saying. He wanted to know if we knew the name of her customer. He wanted a description of him, age, hair, size, all that kind of stuff.

Candy told him that the guy's name was Terry. Or at least that's what he said his name was. She said he was a regular customer, at least once a week. She had been with him once, but after Amber arrived, he always asked for Amber. He had been there maybe five or six times with Amber.

John asked if Amber ever said anything about being with him. The answer was the same from all of us. She said nothing about him or even talked about him after he would leave.

He closed the notebook and stuck it back in his pocket. He talked to Ms. Lee and then she said, "If you think of anything or remember anything. Let me know and I will call John. Girls, this is a very serious matter. Very serious."

Ms. Lee escorted John out of the room and to the back door.

One of the other girls turned to Candy, "What happens to us if they shut us down?"

She replied, "Hard to say. They may move our parlor to a different location. They may move some of us to other parlors but chances are, we would not be with Ms. Lee any longer. It's hard to know what they would do. Either way, they aren't happy about this because they are losing lots of money and she might tell them about the operation."

I asked, "What will they do if they find her first?"

Candy shrugged her shoulders, "Honestly, they'll kill her. If they find her with that guy, they'll kill them both. These people aren't someone that you want pissed off at you. They are very dangerous, very dangerous. And they have lots of power."

Ms. Lee walked back into the room and we all went silent. Nothing else was said about it. I curled up on my bedroll and fell asleep.

I rolled over to see the other girls still sleeping. I got up and went to the restroom. Coming out of the restroom I noticed the door going into the hall was open, as well as the door into the lobby area. I walked to the lobby door and peered into the lobby. The lights were off in the lobby and Ms. Lee was laying on the sofa. I quietly walked to the outside door and peeked through the glass. It was just starting to get light outside.

"Why would she do this?" Ms. Lee asked. "She has no idea what she has done. No idea."

I sat on the end of the sofa and said, "I don't know. Maybe she thought he loved her, so when he asked, she ran away with him. I've had customers tell me that they love me. But I don't think they meant it. I think they said that just hoping I would be nicer to them."

She laughed, "That sounds right. These guys will say anything if they think they can get more for their money."

I asked, "What will happen to us?"

She sat up on the sofa, "I don't know, that depends on if they find her. It depends on who she might talk to. Amber spoke pretty good English, she could say a lot to the wrong people and make it very bad for us. There's nothing we can do but wait and see what happens. In the meantime, Henry wants us to stay closed. Go on, go back to sleep or go watch TV."

I stood up and walking back towards the living area said, "Okay."

Ms. Lee laid down again as I walked away. I went to the laundry room and pulled towels from the dryer and started folding. In my mind, I hoped they didn't find Amber. Maybe she found a way to escape this life. I didn't really like her because of what she had done when I lost my money. But if anyone was able to escape, I wish them the best. I thought about the boy, James. That may have been my only chance to escape, but I lost it.

Two days passed and no word on Amber. There was nothing for us to do during the day. Everything was clean. All the sheets and towels had been cleaned and folded. A couple of the girls spent their time playing some sort of card game. I spent most of the day watching TV or sleeping. One day Ms. Lee ordered pizza to break the boredom. It was a nice change from rice and veggies.

Three days after Amber had left, Henry came to the parlor. When I saw him walk in the living area, the hatred for him and rage boiled in me again. I wanted to jump on him and beat him to death.

I knew that wouldn't happen. He was bigger and stronger than me, but I still festered with the desire to kill him. He talked for a moment with Ms. Lee and then they approached us as we sat on the floor.

He started, "After I leave you can open again. We have lost a lot of money due to Amber's stupidity. I expect you to work extra hard to make it up. I know you think it wasn't your fault she did what she did, but it was. You're supposed to watch each other to be sure these sort of things never happen. When someone does what Amber did, it hurts you all. Get open and get back to work."

He started to walk out when one of the girls asked, "Did they find Amber?"

He turned and walked towards us, pulling something from his pocket. He threw them on the floor in front of us. Pictures, pictures of Amber. At least, it kind of resembled her. She had been beaten so bad that it was hard to tell for sure.

Before anyone could ask, he said, "Yes, she's dead. But we didn't do it. We probably would have, if we had found her. But her boyfriend or whatever he was did it for us. They found her body in a cheap motel on the other side of town. According to my friend John, she had been tortured and beaten to death. The police are looking for him now but John assures me that if he's found. Well, he'll never go to jail or talk to anyone."

He picked up the pictures, putting them back in his pocket, "Let that be a lesson to you. You can't trust your customers. They may tell you anything but they don't care about you. All they care about is the pleasure they can receive from you. You are just a piece of meat to them. Don't forget that!"

He turned and Ms. Lee escorted him out the front door. She turned on the open sign and the lights in the lobby. We were open for business again. There was nothing for us to do but wait for customers.

It was already after noon and a weekday when opened back up. There weren't too many customers that day. Ms. Lee said it would take a while for the word to spread that we were open again.

We all sat in the floor of the living room and talked about Amber. Suzy, the girl that came the same time as Amber, said, "A lot of my customers tell me that they love me. Some even tell me they want to take me away from this. I think, I sometimes believe them and consider it. But no more, I know now. I know they are just lying to get me to pleasure them more, no more."

Candy said, "Yeah, I've had them tell me they want to marry me and give me a good life. I never believed any of what they said. I guess, I've been doing this long enough to know better."

I said in a sad voice, "Yeah, but it is a nice dream. Someone loves you, marries you, moves you into a beautiful house and takes care of you for the rest of your life. It doesn't hurt to dream. Right?"

Suzy said, "Yeah, right. But don't get your hopes to high or dream too much. In the end you'll be hurt. Face it, we are just whores. None of these men want to marry us or love us. Henry said it right. We are just meat for their pleasure."

Our first customer of the day came in the door. Ms. Lee opened the small window to the lobby and greeted him. She opened the door allowing him to come in and started to escort him to one of the massage rooms.

Ms. Lee called out, "Suzy, you're up."

Suzy stood and laughed, "I'll go make him fall in love with me," Leaving the room she said no more.

As she left the room I thought to myself, *it doesn't hurt to have dreams. My dreams are all that keep me going.*

Ms. Lee came into the room, "Rose, come with me."

I got to my feet and followed her into the hallway. She turned to me as I followed her down the hall, "Rose, Henry wanted me to talk to you. He has a client, they call the judge, and he keeps asking for you. Henry has sent other girls to him but he is never happy. He wants you to come see him. Do you remember the judge?"

I replied, "Yes ma'am. He was very weird, but very nice."

She grunted, "Well, he wants you and won't settle for anyone else. Henry has concerns. He knows that you hate him over what happened but he says if he can trust you, he would send you to the judge. Rose, Henry is a very powerful person in this organization. He could do lots of things to make your life better. I don't want to lose you, I like you. But if you could do better, I would be happy. You have to put the past behind you and think of your future. Do you understand what I'm saying?"

"Yes ma'am. I understand. Can I think about it?"

"Sure, that's okay. He wants you to be sure and most importantly, he wants to be sure he can trust you. Think about it." She turned and walked back to the small window when another customer came in the front door.

I hate Henry, but life was better working for him. I didn't have to go with as many men. With Ms. Lee, I may have six or seven customers in a day. With Henry, I would have only one or two in a day, sometimes none. I just didn't know if I could put what happened to Linn behind me. Every time I would think about that incident the anger would boil up in me again.

"Rose, you've got a customer." Ms. Lee yelled.

I went to meet my first customer of the day. Ms. Lee told me he was in room three and to be careful, start slow. She didn't know him and he had never been to the parlor before. I walked into the room and introduced myself to him. He was really tall. His feet almost hung off the end of the table. Not sure, I think he was in his mid-thirties. He had a large tattoo of a snake on his right arm and a spider's web on his left shoulder. I started massaging him and he just lay there. I thought for a while it was only going to be a massage, but I was wrong. Not

139

long into the massage he started suggesting things for me to do, to please him. I didn't hesitate, but did what he requested. I was sure he wasn't a cop or anything of that nature because of the things he did and the things he requested. When we had finished I escorted him to the front and then went back to the room to change the sheets and clean the room. The rest of the day went the same. I had three more customers before closing.

That night I laid on my bedroll thinking to myself, *if I go back to Henry, I will sleep in a nice bed, not on a bedroll on the floor. I won't have to pleasure as many men and some of them, like the judge, don't even want sex. It's just, every time I see Henry I think of Linn and want to kill him. Somehow I would have to hide those feelings from Henry.*

I fell asleep that night thinking about Linn and Henry. I drifted into dreams at different times during the night back with Linn. Sometimes we were just talking and then other times I was back in that room, watching those people cut her and torture her. I never understood why they didn't do the same to me. Poor Linn, I'm sure she suffered a lot of pain before she died. Somehow, someday, I would love to see Henry pay for what he let them do to her for money. I realized that if I went back to him I would never be able to put that behind me. I'd just have to hide my feelings and desires to see him suffer and die.

I didn't get much sleep that night, for thinking about Linn and Henry. I never came to a decision, go with Henry or not.

Candy woke me up saying, "Up and at it sleepyhead. It's Saturday, we'll be busy today. Get up, get up."

I got up, folded my bedroll and went to wash my face and clean up. Just after finishing some breakfast we opened. It wasn't long after that, we had our first customer.

The day had passed by quickly because we were so busy. It was getting close to closing time and I had just escorted my sixth customer to the front. I heard Ms. Lee knocking on one of the doors.

As she knocked, she said, "Candy, his hour is up. You need to finish or he needs to pay more. I think it's been well over an hour. Hurry up"

I was just going into the laundry room with the dirty sheets when I heard Ms. Lee yell, "Oh God, no, no, no!"

I went as fast as I could to the room. Two of the other girls were standing in the doorway in shock. I pushed my way through them. Ms. Lee was sitting on the floor, holding Candy's nude body in her arms. I looked for blood, but seen none. Then I saw the small belt tied around her neck. I reached down to remove the belt and in doing so I felt a pulse in her neck. She was still alive.

I yelled at Ms. Lee, "She's not dead, she's not dead. Ms. Lee, she's not dead."

I pulled the belt off and threw it to the side. I yelled at one of the other girls to bring a wet rag.

I yelled at Ms. Lee," I think her throat is crushed. She's not dead. We have to get help. Call someone! Call Someone!"

Tears flowing down her cheeks she said, "I can't. I can't. She has no ID. She's not legal. I want to but I can't." Looking at Candy, her voice trembled, "Please Candy. Please Candy, don't die."

I could hardly talk, "Please, Ms. Lee, call someone. Please, don't let her die, please."

She jumped up and ran to the front. I sat holding Candy in my arms. I pulled a sheet from under the table and covered her.

With my eyes filled with tears, I rocked back and forth on the floor, holding her tight to my chest, "Candy, please. Candy, please don't die. Please, don't leave me, please, please, not you."

I heard Ms. Lee running down the hall towards us. She came in the room with her cell phone to her ear. She had called someone and was talking to them. I looked up at Ms. Lee but could barely see her through the tears in my eyes.

She cried out, "I can't let her die. I called for an ambulance. Their on the way. She'll be okay. She'll be okay."

"Thank you, thank you, Ms. Lee." I cried.

Suzy, standing in the door, said, "I hear the ambulance. I hear the ambulance. I'll go let them in, okay?"

Ms. Lee replied, "No, No, I'll do it. The police will come too." Looking at me, she said, "Rose, I'm sorry but I want you and the other girls to go to the secret room. I don't want you here when the police come.  You have to go.  Now, please.  I'll make sure she's okay.  When they leave, I'll come and get you.   Go, go, now."

I kissed Candy on the forehead.  I laid her down gently on the floor and put a pillow under her head.  She shocked me by grabbing my hand and squeezing it.  She opened her eyes for the first time since we had found her.  She gasped for air and looked into my eyes.

Ms. Lee bawled, "Go, go, and hurry. Go."

I kissed her hand and then laid it on her chest.  I smiled at her and she closed her eyes again.  Me and the other girls headed for the secret room as Ms. Lee ran to the front.  We pulled the shelf back and were sliding the door shut as I heard people coming down the hall.  While I sat in the dark with the other girls, I found myself praying a silent prayer.  *If there really is a God and if Jesus really loves us.  Please help Candy.  Don't let her die.  She doesn't deserve to die.  Please God or Jesus, let her live, let her live.*

I don't know how long we sat there in the dark.  I know it was a long time before I heard the shelf being pulled from the wall.  Ms. Lee slid the door open and looked at us.

"They took her to the hospital."  With tears streaming down her cheeks, "They think she'll be okay."

The other girls got up and started out of the room.  I lowered my head and silently prayed, *Thank you Jesus. Thank you.*

As I walked past Ms. Lee, she grabbed my arm and pulled me to her.  Hugging me, she whispered in my ear, "Thank you Mei-Lan."  She gently grabbed my head in both her hands and holding me in front of her, looked into my eyes, "Thank you for insisting I call for help. I was scared but I knew you were right. She's been with me longer than any other girl. I don't know that I could live if I would have let her lay there in the floor and die. Thank you."

We embraced each other and then walked towards the front. As we walked to the front, it dawned on me. That was the first time she ever called me Mei-Lan since we first met.

I couldn't sleep that night. I was worried about Candy and wished there was some way to find out how she was doing. Ms. Lee was moving around all night, from worry too. I saw her go out into the lobby area. I hesitated at first, but went out to check on her. She was sitting on the sofa staring out the glass front door. It was late by that time so there wasn't much traffic on the street.

I sat next to her and asked, "Are you okay?"

"Yes, I'm fine. Just have a lot on my mind. Worried about Candy, worried about what Henry will do."

"What's he got to do with this?" I asked.

"Candy has no ID, no passport, she's illegally in America and has been for a long time. The police will be back with lots of questions. She won't be back."

With worry in my voice, I questioned, "Will they put her in a prison camp?'

She let out a small laugh and said, "No, they won't put her in a prison camp. They'll probably send her to a safe home, somewhere far from here."

I asked, "What's a safe home?"

144

"There are organizations in this country that try to help people like Candy and other girls. I'm not supposed to tell you about this, so please tell no one you heard it from me. They help girls, such as Candy, find a better life. Not working in a whorehouse or a massage parlor. They provide them a second chance to have a better life."

I said, "That's good, right?"

"Yes, but it's not easy. Henry and people like him will try to find them and bring them back. He thinks of them, you and me as only property. Win he loses them, he loses money. He's going to be real mad when he finds out that I called an ambulance for Candy."

"What will he do?"

"I don't know, I had to call for her. I couldn't let her die. I couldn't." Tears began to swell in her eyes. "Candy was like a daughter to me. I couldn't let her die. I will never see her again but I know she will be better off than she was here."

She wiped her eyes and got serious, "Mei- Lan, if you ever have the opportunity to escape this lifestyle, don't hesitate. Just be sure you can. If you don't do it right, Henry will look for you. If he finds you, he'll probably put you in one of the low brothels or kill you, after he tortures you. Don't just run away like Amber, have a plan. Be sure he can't find you."

I put my arm around her and asked, "What about you? What will he do to you?"

She smiled and said, "I don't know. He may kill me. At my age, he wouldn't send me to a brothel. No one would want me for pleasure. I don't care. I did what my heart told me to do. Thank you, Mei-Lan. Because of you, I listened to my heart, thank you."

She kissed me on the top of my head and told me to go to bed. I walked back to the living area, leaving her sitting on the sofa. I laid down on my bedroll, not to sleep, because I knew I couldn't. So many thoughts ran through my head. I finally drifted off to sleep but continued to see and think about so many things in my dreams.

During the night, Ms. Lee woke me up, "Mei-Lan, come and lock the lobby door after I leave. Sleep on the sofa until I come back."

Walking into the lobby I asked, "Where are you going?"

She shrugged her shoulders, "I called and found out what hospital they took Candy to."

She paused and then said, "You know, her real name is Son Lee. I gave her the name Candy. That was a long time ago. Anyway, I'm going to go see her and tell someone there about her situation. They have to protect her from Henry. I will have to call him in the morning and tell him what happened. She must be protected."

Ms. Lee went out the door and climbed into a waiting taxi. I locked the door and laid on the sofa. As I laid there, I knew that Candy, Son Lee, was going to be okay.

I looked up at the ceiling and said, "Thank you, Jesus. Please protect Son Lee or Candy, give her the opportunity to have a better life. Jesus, give me strength and help me to somehow escape this life also. Oh, and one more thing. Please take care of my friend Su-Lin. Oh, and also watch over Ms. Lee and protect her from Henry."

I rolled on my side so I could keep my eyes on the door, not planning to sleep. That didn't happen. It wasn't long until I again fell asleep.

# Chapter 15

*I can barely see the image of a face in front of me. The fog is so heavy. I see lights moving in front of me. I hear someone talking to me, but can't understand what's being said. I want to touch the face in front of me, but my hand won't move. I want to look around, but can't move my head. I want to ask, where I'm I? I can't talk, nothing comes out. The lights are going dim and its growing dark, dark and darker. I'm covered with a blanket of darkness.*

"Rose, Rose wake up. Wake up. Rose, wake up."

Someone is pounding on something. Then I hear, "Rose, wake up. Let me in."

I slowly open my eyes to see Ms. Lee at the door. I jump from the sofa and open the door for her. She hurried inside, locking the door behind her.

I asked, "Did you see Candy?"

"Yes, she's going to be okay. She won't be able to talk for a while. The hospital called some lady to talk to me. She came to the hospital and we talked. I told her that Candy's real name is Son Lee. I explained all that I could to her. I told her about Henry, without mentioning his name. She wanted me to stay with them but I convinced her that it would be dangerous for all of you. They are going to move Candy this morning." She began to cry, "I won't ever see her again. That's okay. I know she will be safe and will be free from this life."

I put my arms around her and said, "She'll be okay. Henry won't find her. I know she will be protected. I just worry about what Henry will do to you, when he finds out."

"That's okay. It doesn't matter what is done to me. I don't care anymore. Now, go to bed. It will be light in a few hours. This is going to be a hectic day. I'm sure the police will be back with lots of questions and I'm sure Henry will come also."

I started to walk away when she said, "Rose, this is important. If the police come, you must hide in the secret room. I want you free from here but you are too vulnerable to Henry at this time. Do you understand?'

"Yes, I know what you mean." I turned and went back to the living area and went back to sleep.

She was right. She called Henry at first light and it wasn't long before he was at the door. He told us not to open for a while, he wanted to talk to each one of us. Ms. Lee and Henry went into the laundry room and closed the door. While they were talking, someone was knocking on the front door. Suzy peeked around the corner and then looked back at me.

"Rose, I think it's the police. You better go to the secret room."

Without questioning her I jumped up and ran to the laundry room. I knocked on the door.

I heard Henry, "What? What is it?"

I opened the door and went in. I could see Ms. Lee was crying and the side of her face was very red. I'm sure he had hit her. I told them that the police were at the front door and went to pull the shelf from the room. Henry didn't want to be there when the police were there. He had Ms. Lee let him out the back door. I went into the secret room, pulled the shelf back and slid the door closed. I sat in the dark by myself, thinking about Henry. I hated him so much. Leaning back against the wall, I fell asleep.

A few hours passed, Ms. Lee came and pulled the shelf back and opened the door. She didn't look to happy.

I walked out of the room, "What happened? What did the police do?"

She grunted, "They shut us down for failure to have a license for a massage parlor. Some sort of new law, any business operating as a massage parlor, must be licensed and inspected be the city."

"And so, what now?"

She said, "Henry will get around that. He'll probably just move us to a different location and open under a different name. They are going to notify INS."

"What's INS?" I asked.

"Immigration and Naturalization Service. It's a government agency that deals with people that are illegally in this country. They can take you in to custody, send you back to China, lots of things."

I questioned, "Would that be bad? I'd get to go home."

149

She put her hand on my shoulder, "And do what?  You have no family left there.  You have no money.  No job.  What would you do?  How would you live?"

I thought.  She was right.  There is nothing in Hong Kong for me.  My life there wouldn't be any better.

Her cell phone rang and she held her hand up to me, as if, telling me to wait.  It was Henry, she began telling him what had happened with the police and what they had said.  She listened for a moment, without saying anything.  Laying the phone on the table, she looked at me and said, "He'll be back in a while.  He is going to check on some things.  Probably going to try and find Candy.  He won't find her.  I asked the police lady that was here, with the other policemen, about Candy.  She has already been moved to a safe location out of the city.  That's all she could say about her.  At least, that's good."

With a spring in my voice I said, "Good.  Good, I'm glad she's safe."

She smiled and said, "Me too.  Come on, let's go up front with the other girls."

We all sat in the living area, watching TV, waiting for Henry to come or call.  I thought about the fact, I realized there was nothing, no reason, for me to go back to Hong Kong.  The only family I had ever known about was Dad, Mom and Bo.  If other family members existed, I had no idea, who they are, where they are or anything about them.  There was no reason for me to go back to Hong Kong.  I had nothing to go back to.

150

Ms. Lee's cell phone rang. She answered it and then went to the back door, to let Henry in. He walked into the living area followed by Ms. Lee and two Chinese men. Another Chinese lady, maybe in her late twenties, followed them in and stood next to Henry.

She moved closer to us and looked us over, "My name is Mickey. I work for Henry." She pointed at all the other girls, but not me. "You will all come with me. We are moving you. I have a place in another part of town and you will work there."

They all got up and followed her out the door.

Henry stood there, in silence.

I finally asked, "What about me and Ms. Lee?"

"Don't worry about Ms. Lee. She will be taken care of. This parlor will not reopen. Rose, I am going to give you a choice. You can go to one of the many brothels we have or you can come back with me. I have a few customers, including the judge, that ask about you. I don't know if I can trust you, not to make trouble." He looked me directly in the eyes and said, "Can I trust you? No crap, no problems or would you rather go to a brothel. You'll entertain fifteen to twenty men a day in a brothel. I make money either way. It's your choice."

From what I had been told about the brothels I knew I didn't want to go there. I looked at Ms. Lee. She shook her head as if to say, yes. I looked at him and said, "You. I'll go with you. No problems."

He smiled and said, "Okay."

He took out his cell phone and called someone. I heard him tell them to send a crew today. He wanted the parlor cleaned out today. He said not to worry about the sign but just get the sheets, towels and anything else they could use at another location. I heard the back door slam shut and another Chinese lady came into the living area. She was much older, maybe in her fifties.

Henry told me to gather my stuff and come with him. The lady told Ms. Lee to gather her stuff because she would be going with her. Ms. Lee asked if she could have a moment to tell me goodbye. They told her to make it quick. They wanted to be out of there before more cops or INS came. They walked into the hall and were talking as they went to the back door.

Ms. Lee hugged me and said, "Rose, no, Mei-Lan, We won't see each other again. Take care of yourself and be careful. Remember, be sure of what you are doing, when you do it. Do you know what I mean?"

Crying I said, "Yes, I know. What will happen to you?"

With tears flowing down her cheeks, "Don't worry about me. You worry about you. I have something for you."

She walked to her bedroll and pulled a rolled up towel out and handed it to me. I was in shock when I unrolled it. It was the money I had stashed.

I threw my arms around her, "Wow, thank you. Thank you."

She quietly said, "Put it in your pocket." With that she hugged me tight and told me to take care of myself.

152

My eyes were swollen with tears, "Thank you, Ms. Lee." I hugged her tight and whispered in her ear, "Thank you so much."

She smiled and we walked down the hall, hand in hand. I went out the backdoor and Henry was already in the big black car. The same Chinese guy as before was holding the door open. I waved, goodbye, to Ms. Lee and climbed into the car. As we drove off I looked back to see Ms. Lee standing in the doorway of the parlor with the other Chinese lady. My heart was full of sorrow, I knew, I would never see her again.

As we drove away, I sat back in the seat and thought to myself, *Linn, your time will come. He will pay. Somehow, he will pay. I promise.*

# Chapter 16

Nothing was said as we drove through the city.  We pulled up in front of the same building that I had stayed in before.  The driver got out and opened the door for us.  Henry went out first and then I followed.  I followed Henry through the entry to the elevator.  When the elevator stopped, I followed him into the same apartment.  Cherry, the young girl from the parlor, was curled up on the sofa watching TV.

Seeing me, she screamed, "Rose." She jumped up and ran to me throwing her arms around me. "Wow, I'm glad to see you."

We hugged and then sat together on the sofa.  It gave me a good feeling to see her and to know she was okay.  While we were sitting on the sofa, the bedroom door opened and a very pretty Chinese girl, maybe twenty-five or twenty-six years old, came out of the bedroom.  She smiled at me and walked across the room to the refrigerator.  Popping the top on a soda, she leaned back against the counter and asked, "And who are you?"

Before I could say anything, Henry said, "This is Rose.  She worked for me before.  We had a little problem but I hope it's all okay now.  She was the favorite of the judge."

The girl said, "Oh wow, so you're the Rose. The judge always ask about you. You must have really done something right with him. I'm Diamond. "She laughed, "Maybe I can learn something from you."

She walked back into the bedroom and closed the door.

Henry said, "You should have clothes still in the bedroom. I have things to do and I'll be back later. Oh, one more thing. Do you know anything about Candy or where she might be found?"

In my saddest voice I said, "I thought she died. She didn't make it, did she?"

He grunted and left out the door. It was very hard for me to hide my true feelings. I wanted to yell at him that he would never find her because she is free of him and this life. I wanted to scream at him and tell him how much I hated him for what he had done to Linn. I wanted to yell at him and tell him that his day was coming, he would get his. But, for now, I had to pull a cloak over me in order to hide those feelings. Ms. Lee had said, be sure. I would wait and be sure.

It was such a good feeling to see Cherry again. We sat on the sofa and she told me about some of the customers she had been with. She went to the judge, one time, but all he talked about was how much he had liked Rose. She said he didn't even touch her. She sat and watched TV, while he worked on something. He had Henry pick her up early, didn't even want her to spend the night. I told her about all that had occurred at the parlor. I told her about what happened to Candy but didn't say anything about her going to a safe home. I told her that the

155

parlor had been closed and the other girls went to another parlor. I told her I didn't know what happened to Ms. Lee but I hoped she was okay.

Cherry held my hand and said, "I'm so happy to see you again. I'm glad you came back to here. Diamond's not mean or anything but she doesn't ever talk to me about anything. I know you and I can be good friends."

I smiled and said, "That's good. Yes, we can be good friends."

I had made myself a promise earlier that I didn't want to be close to anyone. I didn't want to be hurt like before but I think I also needed a friend. I did make a decision, sitting on that sofa, if it ever came to protecting her. I would do it with my life, if necessary. I wouldn't let her suffer and be hurt like Linn.

It was hard not to become close to Cherry. She was so young, so sweet, so petite, and so innocent and she had the sweetest smile I had ever seen. We sat for the rest of the day, talking about our families and how we had come to America. Over just a few hours, we became very close. I told her about Su-Lin and her faith in Jesus.

I asked, "Cherry, have you heard about the guy named Jesus?"

"Yeah, but I don't know a lot about him. No one ever really told me much about him. I know he wasn't Chinese."

I laughed, "No, he wasn't Chinese. Not sure where he was from but I think he was white." I proceeded to tell her what I knew about him. "He was the son of God, he lived a long time ago. He was put on a cross, where he died. They say he died for us because he loves us so much.  The story says, three days after he died, he came back to life.  From what I understand, he ascended into a place called heaven, but not before saying, he was going to be with the father and prepare a home for us with his father in the place called heaven.  Su-Lin told me all of that.  She said he loves us no matter what we have done.  She really believed those words."

Cherry listened and asked, "How did she know all of that about him?"

"Her Mom and Dad had taught her and she had a little book, called a bible, that told all about him.  She read that book all the time. She gave it to me just before she died." I lowered my head and sadly said, "I lost it when I first came to America."

She shook her head and said, "That's too bad."

"Yeah, but I didn't know how to read anyway.  But I think that knowing about him has given me strength.  I believe the things I've heard about him."

Diamond walked from the bedroom and we quit talking.  She was dressed real fancy and looked so beautiful.

She told us that we were on our own for a while.  She had a customer to go see and Henry was going to pick her up downstairs.  She said, "You know the rules, no stupid stuff."

She walked out the door, closing it behind her.

After she left, nothing else was said about Jesus.  We started looking through the counter looking for food.  After finding two cups of ramyon noodles, we had a feast, sitting on the sofa watching TV.

157

After finishing my noodles, I went through the bedroom to the restroom. I closed the door, opened the cabinet under the sink. There was a box of what looked and smelled like some sort of bath powder that had been there for a long time. It looked like it had not been used in a while. I took the money from my pocket, counted out over a thousand dollars, and then stuffed it deep in the box of powder.

It was late that night when Diamond returned. She told me to get some sleep because I was going to see the judge in the morning. Henry had called the judge and told him that I was back. Henry said the judge was ecstatic and wanted to see me the next morning.

I said, "Okay." Got up and went to the bedroom, followed by Cherry. Cherry and I shared the same bedroom that I had shared with Linn, Diamond was in the other bedroom. It didn't take long for Cherry to fall asleep. I lay next to her in the big bed, lots of thoughts ran through my mind. I thought about Linn and the rage started to build in me again but something else seemed to push that aside. A calm came over me, I realized it was Jesus. I knew he was with me, no matter what happened. I knew, with all my heart, he had answered my prayer for Candy. I knew that Henry would never find her because Jesus would watch over her and protect her. Maybe James had helped her. I had a warm feeling come over me as I thought about her. It didn't take long for me to relax and fall asleep.

The next morning I awoke feeling good. Cherry was still sleeping when I got out of the bed and walked into the living room. Diamond was sitting on the sofa, sipping on a cup of coffee. I walked to the fridge, pulling out a bottle of water. I sat in the chair across from the sofa.

Diamond looked at me and asked, "What is it with you and Henry? Last night, coming home, I could sense that he's a little scared of you. He was on the phone, the whole trip, talking to someone about a girl named Candy. He wants to find her in a really bad way. Do you know anything about her?"

I replied, "She worked at the same massage parlor I worked at. A few days ago, she was hurt real bad by a customer. The mamasan at the parlor called for an ambulance. They took her to the hospital." I thought for a moment, "The last thing I heard was, she didn't make it. She died at the hospital."

"Well, Henry apparently doesn't believe that. His connections on and off the police department can't find anything about her, no body, nothing. I think, he thinks she is still alive and someone is hiding her. I've never seen him in such a mood, as he is over this."

I said, "I don't know. I thought she died."

She snickered, "She must know a lot about Henry and his operation. He wants to find her and he's for sure that you know more than you're saying. I heard him tell someone on the phone about some old lady, I think, named Ms. Lee."

I asked, "What did he say about her?"

"I only heard one side of the conversation but I think they beat and tortured her. I don't think she told them anything. Henry wasn't too happy about that. I think they killed her."

My heart sunk and sorrow flooded through my soul. I fought to hold back the tears. I didn't want Diamond to see me crying.

159

I shook my head and said, "That's too bad. I have to go to the restroom."

I went through the bedroom, Cherry was still sleeping as I went in the bathroom and closed the door, locking it behind me. I sat on the toilet seat and lowered my head into my hands. The flood of tears started. I thought, *poor Ms. Lee, they killed her and gained nothing from it. These people are nothing but monsters. How could they do this way to other people? I was sure Ms. Lee told them nothing. She protected Candy to the death. Henry must be afraid that Candy would tell all she knows about Henry and his operation. I am the last connection he has to Candy. I have to continue to tell them I know nothing.*

I wiped the tears from my eyes and prayed quietly, "Jesus, I know you hear me. I know you heard my prayer, before, about Candy and you answered it by protecting her. I'm going to need your strength. I don't care what happens to me now but I have to find a way to bring Henry down. Please help me to do that. Su-Lin told me that all things are possible through you and she really believed that. Watch over Candy and give her a good life."

"Rose, I need to use the bathroom!" Cherry knocking on the door.

I wiped my eyes and washed my face in the sink and opened the door. She rushed past me to the toilet. I walked back into the living room and Diamond was talking on her cell phone.

She hung up and said, "That was Henry. He says for you to get cleaned up, put on the school uniform and put your hair in pigtails. He will be around in a few hours to pick you up."

I walked into the small kitchen area and scooped a bowl full of rice from the rice maker. Standing at the counter, eating the rice, I wondered what Diamond had told Henry. He may have told her to question me about Candy.

160

When Henry arrived, I was dressed and ready to go.  He smiled and said, "Good. Very Good.  The judge will be pleased. Let's go."

During the drive very little was said, until I asked, "Do you get a lot of money for what we do?"

It shocked him but he answered, "Yes, that's why I take such good care of you.  Honestly, it's all about money.  The judge and people like him are willing to pay a lot for your services and my discretion. So, yes, you and all the girls are worth a lot of money to me.  That's why I need to find Candy.  She can hurt all of us."

I thought to myself, *you mean she can hurt you.*  Then I said, "I don't know how she can hurt you.  She's dead. Right?"

He said nothing else but just looked out the window.  I didn't say another word but knew he wasn't happy with my remark.

We pulled up in front of the same fancy hotel, where I had met the judge before.  The driver opened the door and I followed Henry out.  Nothing was said until we walked into the suite.  The judge was standing on the balcony when we got off the elevator to his suite.  He rushed over and threw his arms around me.  After holding me for a few minutes, he pulled a very thick envelope from his pocket and gave it to Henry.

Henry said, "Thank you and just give me a call later, if you want her to stay for the night."

The judge just nodded yes.  Henry turned and went back in the elevator.  The judge

pulled me to him again, wrapping his arms around me, he said, "I'm so glad to see you.  I've

missed you so much."

I thought for a moment and said, "I missed you too, daddy."

With that he hugged me even tighter.  He grabbed my hand and led me to the balcony.

Pointing at the table he said, "Look, I have your favorite."

A large bowl of beautiful strawberries was setting on the table.  He pulled the chair out

for me to sit and then he sat across from me.  I picked up one of the strawberries and plopped

it into my mouth. He smiled as he watched me eat it.

I reached across and touched his hand, "Thank you daddy.  It's good." Honey had

coached me good.

He had a smile from ear to ear.  He began talking to me, but I couldn't understand most

of what he said.  I just ate the strawberries, would look at him and smile.  He would smile back

and keep talking.  When the strawberries were gone, he took me by the hand and led me into

the living room.  He turned on the TV, it was an animated movie about a chicken, trying to fly.  I

sat on the sofa while he sat at a desk making calls and working on something.

It was really strange because the day was almost an exact repeat of the last time I was

with him.  He spanked me for spilling a coke and put me to bed.  He stroked my hair, telling me

how sorry he was and how much he loved me, while I lay under the covers on the bed. It was

almost dark out when he came back in the bedroom.  He led me, by the hand, back to the balcony.  The table was covered with dishes of fruit and boiled shrimp.  I sat down when he pulled the chair out for me.  He treated me like I was his daughter.  It made me wonder if he had a daughter and something happened to her.  I just went along with what he did and every now and then called him daddy and told him I loved him.  I guess he had called Henry, he never came to pick me up that night.  There were no more spankings.  We sat together on the sofa until late that night watching TV. He had me lay with my head in his lap.  He stroked my hair and every so often I would look up at him, call him daddy and tell him I loved him. He would just smile back and keep stroking my hair.  It was late when he led me back to the bed.  After pulling the covers over me, he kissed me on the forehead and told me goodnight.

I looked at him and said, "Goodnight, Daddy."

I didn't sleep well that night.  My sleep was invaded with lots of bad dreams.  I dreamed about Bo, Su-Lin and Linn.  I dreamed that Henry was chasing me and shouting that he would kill me if he caught me.

*The fog is really thick.  I can barely see lights in the fog.  I think I can hear people talking, but again, I'm unable to understand what they are saying.  I want to get some ones attention, so I try to call out, but nothing comes out.  I try to raise my hand to get their attention, but I can't move my hand.  It is getting dark, darker and now I am covered with a blanket of darkness.*

# Chapter 17

I went straight to the restroom after waking up in the morning. I listened, but heard

nothing. I kept expecting the judge to come in the room, but he didn't. The door was open to

the living room so I stepped quietly and peeked in the living room. It was empty, he was gone.

I found a bottle of water and sat on the sofa. It wasn't long before Henry's driver came off the

elevator.

He looked around and said, "Let's go."

I followed him into the elevator and then out to the car waiting in front. He opened the

door and I climbed in the car. Henry was sitting in the car talking on his cell phone. I said

nothing as I sat next to him. The door closed and shortly we started moving. He finished his

phone call and sat in silence.

Nothing was said all the way back to the apartment. We pulled up in front of the

apartment. The driver opened the door and escorted me back upstairs to the apartment.

Henry stayed in the car and never said a word.

Entering the apartment, I found Diamond and Cherry sitting on the sofa watching TV. They asked me how it went with the judge. I told them about what had happened and they agreed that he was a very weird man. I excused myself to go take a shower. After the shower I found Diamond sitting on the bed in our bedroom.

She looked at me and said, "We need to talk."

I questioned, "What's up?"

"I don't particularly care for or like Henry, he scares me. Right now he scares me more than ever before. He was over here for a long time today, drilling me and Cherry. He wanted to know everything that you talked about, especially anything about that girl, Candy. We told him that you said she was dead. He doesn't believe that. He told us that if he found out we were lying or hiding anything from him he would kill us. He believes that you know more than what you are saying. You had better watch your back."

I said, "I already told him just like I'm telling you. She is dead and that's all I know. What else can I say? There's nothing else."

She got up and started walking back to the living room, "Even if that's true. Watch your back. He doesn't believe you. And he really wants Candy in the worst way."

I sat on the edge of the bed thinking about what she had said. What could he do to me? He could torture me. He could even kill me. I will never change my story about Candy. I don't care what he does to me. I hope that Candy talks and tells them everything she knows. They will come after him and that would be great. It would give me a good feeling to see him go down.  I walked into the living room and sat on the sofa next to Diamond and Cherry.  Henry never came back and never called Diamond.  We sat watching TV, worked together fixing supper and then we all went to bed.

Laying in the bed next to me Cherry asked, "Are you Okay?"

I replied, "Sure, why not?"

"I thought maybe you were worried about Henry.  I know Diamond told you about him coming here today and what he said."

I rolled over and looked at her.  I smiled and said, "I'm not worried.  What can he do to me?  Sure, he could kill me but I'm not scared to die.  I know now, if I die, I go to a better life.  I will go to be with Su-Lin and Jesus in heaven.  I have no doubt it would be better than the life I've had for the last few years.  Yeah, I'm okay."

She didn't hear a word I said.  She had already fell to sleep. I rolled over and let sleep take over.

We didn't hear anything from Henry until the following day.  He called and told Diamond to have us both, Cherry and myself, to be ready at about dark. He said he had appointments for us at the same time with two different customers in the same hotel.

I thought, *he must be happy about that.  Double money at the same time and not as much travel.*

We were sitting on the sofa when he came for us.  He was all smiles and in a good mood.  It kind of worried me to see him like that.

He said, "Let's go." He escorted us down the elevator and to the waiting car. As always, the driver stood holding the door open for us.

Nothing was said as we drove across the city. Pulling up in front of a very large hotel, we stopped and the driver came and opened the door. Henry exited first and then Cherry and I followed. I looked up, it was a very tall building. Walking through the lobby, I knew this was a place only for the very wealthy. A lady in a hotel uniform and a man dressed in a suit, standing behind a counter, greeted us as we walked through the lobby. I noticed that the man had some sort of badge on his jacket. A few other people were standing around talking.

Going into the elevator, I noticed the panel light was lit up on *L*. Henry's driver had stayed with the car, only Henry, Cherry and myself rode the elevator up. I saw Henry push the number *12 on* the elevator panel. When the elevator stopped, we stepped into a hallway and started walking towards a door at the far end of the hallway. Henry knocked on the door that was numbered *1204.* I heard someone inside say something.

Henry turned to me and said, "We'll drop Cherry first and then I'll take you to yours."

Henry opened the door and we followed him in. It was a very large room with big furniture, a bar on one side and a large TV on the other side. There was a door on one side of the room next to the bar. I figured it went into a bedroom. There was no one in the room. We stood, in silence, waiting for someone to come in the room. Henry stood behind us and said nothing. The door to the bedroom opened and she walked out. My heart dropped and I began to shake. It was the girl. She killed Linn. I panicked and started to back away from her.

Henry wrapped his arms around me, "Remember her?"

I was unable to break free, he held me in a vice like grip. She walked towards me, stroking Cherry's hair as she passed her.

She stopped directly in front of me and gently rubbed the back of her hand down my face, and in perfect Chinese, she said, "Are you ready to have some more fun, sweetie? We're going to have a good time."

Henry whispered in my ear, "New choice, tell me where Candy's at. Tell me everything or watch Cherry suffer just like Linn."

I screamed at the top of my voice, "Cherry, run. Run!"

Before she could move, the girl grabbed her and started pulling her into the bedroom.

I yelled, "No, No!"

The same guy as before stepped from the bedroom and helped take Cherry into the bedroom. I could hear Cherry crying and yelling as they forced her into the room.

Henry held me in his grip, "Now what bitch? I knew I could do nothing to you to make you talk. But you will talk to save Cherry. Tell me where she is and we can all go home. Where's Candy?"

I yelled, "Please, Candy is dead. She died."

He released his grip on me and threw me on the floor in front of the bar. I could hear Cherry screaming in the other room.

The white girl came from the bedroom and in Chinese said, "You ready to play?"

She grabbed me by the hair and started pulling me to my feet. I kicked at her as hard as I could. The toe of my shoe hit her on the inside of her thigh. She released my hair and fell to the floor in pain. From the corner of my eye, I saw Henry coming at me from the rear. I grabbed a large bottle of liquor from the bar counter and swung with everything I had. It connected with the side of his head and broke. As he grabbed his head, I pushed him back. He fell over a chair and I headed for the door. I jerked the door open and ran into the hallway. I had to find someone to help us. I remembered the man in the lobby with the badge on his jacket as the elevator door opened. An older couple walked out and I dashed for the elevator. Henry was running from the room as the elevator door closed. My heart was racing and sweat and tears ran down my face. I had to find help. I hit the button marked *L.* It seemed like an eternity before the door opened into the lobby. I ran into the lobby screaming in Chinese. I stopped, Henry's driver was running in the front entry door of the lobby. I saw the American man in the suit running from the lobby counter towards us. He was yelling something at us as I saw Henry's driver pull the gun from his jacket. I turned to run back from him, the elevator door opened and Henry, with blood on his face ran from the elevator. I heard the roar of the gun as it went off, then another and another.

Henry grabbed me and pulled me to him. I saw the gun in his hand and then I felt it, before I heard it. A hot fire suddenly burned through my chest. I felt it again as he shot me again. He held me tight with his hand and looked into my face. Suddenly his head exploded in front of me and he dropped me to the floor. I could hear people screaming and yelling all around me. The guy in the suit and some lady knelt beside me.

169

I gathered all the strength in me I could and screamed in English, "One-two-zero-four. One-two-zero-four, please help, please help her. Help Cherry."

I heard the man yell at someone, "Hurry, hurry, 1204."

I laid my head back on the floor and turned it to the side. Henry was staring at me with his eyes wide open and an expression of shock on his face. Blood was all around him, the side of his head was gone. My promise had been fulfilled, he got his. I could hear sirens and lots of commotion around me. I felt myself slipping away.

I felt someone touch my head and heard, "Rose, I'm here. I'm here. I'm okay."

It was Cherry, she was okay. I couldn't open my eyes or lift my head to look at her. That was okay, she was safe. I felt myself slip away.

*There's fog all around me. I hear people talking. I want to scream, where am I? But can't. I try to move, but can't. Now I see an image of a face in front of me. I hear a voice, in Chinese, "Mei-Lan, its James. I am here. I've looked everywhere for you. You're safe and the little girl called Cherry is safe. We moved her to a safe place, she'll be okay."*

*I felt him hold my hand as he said, "You've been shot twice in the chest. Henry and his driver were both killed in the gun battle. Thanks to you and Candy a lot of girls have been rescued. You were so brave. We're going to get you through this, you'll be okay."*

*I heard him start to pray, "Precious Jesus, please be with Mei-lan and help her to recover. Be with her and bless her."*

*His image and his voice begin to fade. I can't see him anymore. All I see is fog and a bright light in the fog. I see a girl walking towards me through the fog. She reaches out her hand for me and says, "Mei-Lan, my friend, my sister, I am here to take you home."*

*The fog clears as she stands in front of me with her outstretched hand and a smile on her face. I reach to her and take her hand. Su-Lin takes me home.*

# Epilogue

Mei-Lan's story, even though fictional, is a small example of a worldwide crisis. Human trafficking is the third largest and most lucrative enterprise in the world behind drug smuggling and arms dealing. The U.S. Department of State estimates that 15,000 to 17,000 people are trafficked into the U.S. every year. 50% of those trafficked are children. 80% of the people trafficked into the U.S. are forced into prostitution while the other 20% are held as slaves in domestic servitude. CAST {Coalition to Abolish Slavery and Trafficking) estimates that there are over 10,000 women held in underground brothels across California. The largest source of people trafficked are from Asia. The average age of a girl or boy forced into prostitution in the U.S. is 12 to 14 years old and their life expectancy is only to about 17 years of age. We as humans and especially as Christians must not remain neutral. We must take a stand as prayer warriors. Get involved in the fight against the crime of human trafficking and try to make a difference.

The trafficker, for financial gain, steals the lives and dreams of young children. We ask, so many times, why? God granted us the gift of free will, to make our choices on how we lead our lives. Sadly, there are those in the world, due to the influence of Satan, that choose to make choices that create hardships, pain and suffering for other people.

The bible tells us in so many words that children have a special place in God's heart.

The American New Revised Version Bible, Matthew 18 reads: *At that time the disciples came to Jesus and said, "Who then is greatest in the kingdom of heaven?"  And Jesus called a child to himself and set him before them, and said, "Truly, I say to you, unless you are converted and become like children, you will not enter the kingdom of heaven.  Whoever then humbles himself as this child, he is the greatest in the kingdom of heaven.  And whoever receives one such child in my name receives me. But whoever causes one of these little ones, who believe in me to stumble, it would be better for him to have a heavy millstone hung around his neck, and to be drowned in the depth of the sea."*

## Get involved!

www.ingramcontent.com/pod-product-compliance
Lightning Source LLC
Chambersburg PA
CBHW080805120626
46556CB00009B/3235